The Machination of Vipers

ROBERT DWIGHT BROWN

The Machination of Vipers

Full Color & Illustrated - Green Letter Edition
With the Words the False Prophet, the Dreamer of Dreams in Green
& God the Father in Purple

Allonymous Books
A Division of Chi Xi Stigma Publishing Company, LLC

Dedicated to the Questioners of the Christ
From Friedrich Nietzsche & Karl Marx
To Ayn Rand, Richard Dawkins & Saul of Taurus
Through your inspiration, I question the
Good News of Jesus the Christ through
The Unreliable Narration of the Vipers!

Allonymous Books

A Division of Chi Xi Stigma Publishing Company, LLC

Trade Paperback— ISBN 13: 978-1-931608-71-8

Also Available: *The Harrowed Heart* **— ISBN 13: 978-1-931608-48-0**
Also Available: *The First Exorcist* / *The Harrowing of the Inferno*
                      — ISBN 13: 978-1-931608-60-2

Cover image: Jodaens, Jacob, *Christ Driving the Money Changers from the Temple,* c. 1650, Louvre
     Museum, Paris, France
Paper image:: http://www.myfreetextures.com/vintage-paper-texture-with-design/

The New Testament Remixed:

The art of the remixing one artist's popular song by another artist/ producer or the art of "sampling" in the hip-hop parlance of the late 1970's and 80's is lost on most people whom were not reared in the housing projects of the Bronx and other New York City boroughs. There block parties were hosted by the legendary likes of DJ Kool Herc, gave birth to an art-form predicated on the taking of the percussion "breaks" from one record and mixing it with the "breaks" of another record. This became known as sampling. As hip-hop evolved, so did the technology, allowing producers to take elements of various songs and mixing them together to make an entirely new song. This has proven to be highly controversial in the music industry (despite, or because of the profitability of the new work). The art of sampling continues to line the coffers of lawyers who argue the multitudinous lawsuits over copyright infringement. Where does one person's art (and property) end and another's art (and property) begin? That is one of the great questions raised by the rise of hip-hop.

Alan Moore's *The League of Extraordinary Gentlemen,* a series of comic-book miniseries, is a **remix (or sampling)** of literary main characters from novels *Dracula, King Solomon's Mines, 20,000 Leagues Under the Sea, The Strange Case of Dr. Jekyll and Mr. Hyde, The Invisible Man, Orlando: A Biography,* and *Carnacki the Ghost-Finder* (all fallen into the public domain, conveniently).

The Holy Bible by its very structure is a literary **remix (or sampling)**. It's sixty-six books (according to Protestant Reformers) are each the individual works of human authors (howbeit a single divine Author). Each of the books stand on their own as individual works, but only when bound together into the **remix** called the Holy Bible, do they transcend the written word to become the Word of **God**.

The Old Testament is itself a **remix** of Hebrew oral and written traditions and foreign mythologies. The Torah, once believed to be the work of a single author, namely Moses, is actually a **remix** of the independent authorships of the Jahwist, the Elohist, the Deuteronomist, and the Priestly sources. The other authors of the Old Testament took entire stories, prayers, and covenants from other older Hebrew scripture and freely inserted them into their own books, sometimes with nary a change to be found. Was this outright theft? Or was it a divine **remix**?

The New Testament is also an abuser of this type of divine literary **remix**. The Gospels of Matthew and Luke have been rightly accused by the most esteemed Biblical scholars over the centuries to have plagiarized wantonly the Gospel of Mark and the mysterious Q-"Gospel", creating three "synoptic" Gospels out of an original two (one having been forever lost to history). Only John's Gospel escapes this abuse of **remix** by writing an inherently original and at times throughout history, questioned Gospel. So much for originality.

Doubt me?

Choose any Study Bible worth its salt and you will discover a column of scriptural references for practically every verse in the entirety of the Old and New Testaments. While some of these references are merely thematic in nature, many are paraphrased and often direct quotations of other, older scripture. This is the nature of The Holy Bible: the Divine **Remix**.

Need I continue?

If Jesus, as many Atheists assert, was the fictional creation of his "followers", then the authors of the New Testament made the Gospel of "Jesus of Nazareth" a **remix** of the Messianic prophecies of their Hebrew scripture. If Jesus was either a historical person or the divine, then His ministry is a **remix** of Old Testament and wholly (Holy) original belief systems.

Could I take the texts of the Gospels of Matthew, Mark, Luke, and John and by cutting and pasting scriptures wantonly here and there, compose a truly original work? A horror novel?

Hell, yeah!

Author's Note:

The Green Letter Edition &

The Unreliable Narrator:
In my Red Letter Edition of *The Harrowed Heart*, I choose to put the **spurious** words attributed to Jesus from Gnostic sources (the reviled "Gospels" of Judas and the Infancy Thomas) in a vile, unsettling **green lettering**. This is in stark contrast to the exquisite beauty of the Red Letters of many Holy Bibles that choose to revere the Words of Jesus the Christ. The Pharisaic narrator in *The Machination of Vipers* considers *every* word that comes from Jesus' mouth to be **spurious**, hence the choice to make this a **Green Letter Edition**. It is my hope that seeing the Words of Jesus printed in a vile **green lettering** will turn your stomach, creating a sense of unease and paranoia unique to this *Gospel of Biblical Paranoia*.

Could I employ an unreliable narrator in a Gospel narrative? To the faithful, the narrators of the Gospels are not merely Matthew, Mark, Luke, and John, but God Himself and therefore the most reliable narrator possible. To the atheist, to the skeptic, and to certain Biblical scholars, Matthew, Mark, Luke, and John, being not just evangelists but The Evangelists, are inherently unreliable because they are faithful Disciples of Jesus the Christ and not dispassionate historians. How reliable can they be if they *want* Jesus to be the Messiah, the Son of God? How can the more supernatural elements of the ministry of Jesus, the cures, the exorcisms, the supernatural control over nature, and the resurrections of the dead be explained as anything other than as fantasy? The Gospels are *both* reliable and unreliable depending on your certain point-of-view.

Luke the Physician prefaces his Gospel as a *declaration of those things which are most surely believed among us, even as they delivered them unto us, which from the beginning were eyewitnesses, and ministers of the word* (Lk. 1:1-2). I chose to preface *The Machination of Vipers* as a Gospel narrative from the point-of-view of a Pharisee whom has implanted himself into the discipleship of this certain itinerant Nazarene preacher. My Pharisee is a somewhat passive observer reporting on the words and deeds of the Nazarene in a document intended for the Sanhedrin. It would be accurate, though skeptical, bordering on blasphemous (at least to a Christian). He would use the very scripture to refute the message and ministry of the Nazarene.

—That is until Gene Wolfe passed away and I read a *The New Yorker* article on his life and work, most importantly his *The Book of The New Sun* series. I was greatly intrigued by the narrator, Severian, whom is described as being both a reliable *and* an unreliable narrator. While I already knew the concept of the "unreliable narrator", it wasn't until I read this article that my narrator changed for the better (or worse, depending on your point-of-view)—

Instead and in order to be an unreliable narrator to what extent would (or could) my Pharisee be unreliable and be inaccurate? He would distort, misrepresent, deceive, and toutright fabricate in his reporting to the Sanhedrin. The non-Christian, the lapsed Christian, and even the devout, but unread Christian may *not* be able to readily discern which scriptural verses in *The Machination of Vipers* are unreliable, inaccurate, distorted, misrepresented, deceitful, and outright fabricated. Hopefully, the well-read Christian will instantly identify *all* of the unreliable narration, but also understand *why* I chose an unreliable, inaccurate, distorting, misrepresenting, deceiving, and outright fabricating Pharisaical narrator.

But *why*?

Whether the Gospel in question is one of the Canonical four or a *fifty*-odd Gnostic Gospels, their adherents, who revered the particular (and in some cases peculiar) Gospel, believed the Good News contained within was the inerrant Word of God and the Truth (from their ideological point-of-view). *Why* would I choose to write a Gospel so intent on deceiving the reader? *Why not?!?*

This is not a flippant response, although at first glance it is flippant. The very concept of this book in the **Gospels of Biblical Horror Trinity** is psychological horror. And an integral aspect of psychological horror is paranoia. And no class in the traditional Gospel narrative are nearly as paranoid as the Pharisees and Sadducees. These are the persons that had the most to lose if the prophesied Messiah were to appear and usher in the Kingdom of God. These religious leaders cared more for their own personal power and wealth gifted to them by Rome, than they did their faith in the **LORD God of Israel**. They acted politically, not piously. And this is where the paranoia lies. This is the source of the *psychological horror*.

Of Vipers & Men: "I hear the voice of God!"

Those words have only ever been uttered by prophets or madman. In their own time, every prophet was considered a madman. For every actual prophet, there are countless madmen. For every authentic scripture, there are countless apocrypha. Every believer is but a drop in the sea of skepticism. The whole of Israel chose to worship the Golden Idol while Moses communed with God Himself. Christians were thrown to the lions because their belief in Jesus Christ did not allow them to acknowledge the divinity of Cæsar. Muhammad fought a bloody war with the infidels of Mecca, before his conquest of Arabia, transforming it with the word of Allah: the Quran.

Prophets, of course, can and do, but can a madman put pen to paper and write down the words he heard, the visions he saw, and the dreams he dreamt?

Can a paranoid schizophrenic actually hear the voice of God?

I understand paranoias intimately. Over a quarter-century of psychotherapy has gotten me in touch with my own psychosis and paranoias... intimately. My hallucinations are queerly religious. I see and hear demons, angels, the prophets, apostles, and saints. And I hear the Voice of God. My paranoias are also religious in nature (yet strangely also involve alternate parallel realities as postulated by theoretical physicists). I, of course, dismissed all of these as nothing more than a Catholic paranoid schizophrenic's rather imaginative hallucinations. But the weight of my psychosis has been brought to bare as a heavy cross on my shoulders.

Can a paranoid schizophrenic actually hear the voice of God?

To atheists of the modern era and the Pharisees and Sadducees of the much more ancient one, Jesus of Nazareth of the Galilee was a madman. If one were to psychoanalyze Jesus of Nazareth one would find:

• Social/occupational dysfunction: **He** is a poor and itinerant preacher, who believes he is not only the **Son of God**, but **He** is God (The entirety of the New Testament!).

• Visual hallucination: **He** sees *the heavens open unto* **Him** *and* **He** *saw the* **Spirit of God** *descending like a dove, and lighting upon* **Him** (Mt. 3:16).

- Auditory hallucination: **He** hears *a voice from heaven saying, This is my **Son**, in whom I am well pleased* (Mt. 3:17).
- Visual hallucination: **He** prayed to **His** Father in the Garden of Gethsemane *and there appeared an angel unto him from heaven, strengthening Him* (Lk. 22:43).
- Paranoid delusion (or delusion of persecution): **He** was paranoid that the *Jews would seek the more to kill **Him**, because **He** not only had broken the sabbath, but said also that God was **His** Father, making **Himself** equal with God* (Jn. 7:1).
- Delusion of inflated worth: **He** states emphatically that *He can do nothing of **Himself**, but what **He** seeth the Father do: for what things soever **He** doeth, these also doeth the **Son** likewise* (Jn. 5:19).
- Delusion of knowledge: **He** says God *sheweth **Him** all things that **Himself** doeth* (Jn. 5:20).
- Delusion of power: **He** says if *the Father raiseth up the dead*, **He** can as well (Jn. 5:21).
- Delusion of identity: **He** says God *hath committed all judgment unto the **Son*** (Jn. 5:22).
- Delusion of special relationship with a deity: **He** says that *all men should honour the **Son**, even as they honour the father* (Jn. 5:23).

All the classic symptoms of paranoid schizophrenia, with delusions of grandeur, are present in just a handful of verses.

But to me, source of the paranoia that fuels this psychological horror novel is **_not_** Jesus of Nazareth, **_but_** the Pharisees and Sadducees. They paranoid over the growing influence and authority of an itinerant preacher over the peoples of Judea and the Galilee *and they watched him, and sent forth spies, which should feign themselves just men, that they might take hold of his words, that so they might deliver him unto the power and authority of the governor* (Lk. 20:20). The disciples of this itinerant preacher were paranoid over attention the Pharisees and Sadducees paid to their Rabbi and their influence over the governor: Pontius Pilate.

Paranoias are a strangely cyclical phenomenon feeding upon your fears of others to grow and therefore feeding the paranoias of the others' fear in you. Fear of the growing influence in the opposition feeds their own paranoias and this growth feeds the paranoias of the opposition and this growth feeds their own paranoias until there is an eruption of bile and violence.

Prologue
"Learned in the Law"

OSEPH OF ARIMATHEA WAS IN council with the teachers of the Temple of Jerusalem, during the Feast of Passover, when a young **Boy** sought the same council with them.

And for three days, the **Boy** listened to them and asked questions of them. Joseph and the other teachers were astonished at **His** understanding and **His** answers. Some amongst the teachers tried to trick the **Boy** with deceitful questions, but **His** knowledge of the Law as given by Moses Lawgiver and the Word were great.

On the first day, the **Boy** listened quietly; as the day wore on until the ninth hour Joseph posed a question to the **Boy**, "What is the greatest of all commandments of the LORD?" And the **Boy** answereth, "**The greatest of all commandments in the Law is, 'Thou shalt love the LORD**

1

thy God with all thy heart, and with all thy soul, and with all they mind.' "

And Joseph asked, "Why is it the most difficult commandment to keep." The **Boy** said, **"A man believes the decrees wrought by a king because he believes the words that he hears from the mouth of his king. But this same man can deny, quite easily, the Word of God through his very elucidation of the Word of God."**

The second day began when a teacher posed to interpret the Law: "Thou shalt give life for life, an eye for an eye, a tooth for a tooth. Hand for hand, foot for foot, burning for burning, wound for wound, stripe for stripe." The **Boy** stood before them and said unto the teachers, **"I know what the Word and the Law say, but I say unto you, if an evil-doer strike thee upon your right cheek, turn and offer him the other cheek."**

There was a great murmur in the Temple as the teachers protested the boy's interpretation of the scripture. One young teacher, Caiaphas, stood and demanded the **Boy** leave their presence if the **Boy** refused to accept the scripture as come form the mouth of **God**.

Joseph of Arimathea sat quietly, with his hand upon his chin stroking his chin-whiskers, and pondered the truth in the **Boy's** words. Then finally Joseph spoke to the other teachers in the Temple, "There is truth in the words of this young **Boy**. If this evil-doer, who stuck thee upon thy left cheek, is so full of wrath that he turns his hand to strike thee with his back of his hand upon thy right cheek, a pox be upon him, for which a Jew is wont not to strike thus. And if desire to strike thee remains in his heart, then by offering him your left cheek, you force this evil-doer to strike thee in a manner full of shame." Joseph then invited the **Boy** to stay and the **Boy** turned to Joseph and smiled.

On the third day, the **Boy** again found in the Temple those that sold oxen and sheep and doves, and the changers of money sitting. **He** wished to maketh a scourge of small cords, and driveth them all out of the temple, and the sheep, and the oxen; and pour out the changers' money, and overthrew the tables; and desired to saith unto them that sold doves, **"Take these things hence; make not My Father's house an house of merchandise."** But **His** hour was not yet come.

When the **Boy** then sought council with the teachers, the **Boy** said, **"I would very much like to share a nursery story: there was a certain householder, which planted a vineyard, and hedged it round about, and digged a winepress in it, and built a tower, and let it out to husbandmen, and went into a far country: and when the time of the fruit drew near, he sent his servants to the husbandmen, that they might receive the fruits of it.**

"And the husbandmen took his servants, and beat one, and killed another, and stoned another. Again, he sent other servants more than the first: and they did unto them likewise. But last of all he sent unto them his son, saying, 'They will reverence my son.'

"But when the husbandmen saw the son, they said among themselves, 'This is the heir; come, let us kill him, and let us seize on his inheritance.' And they caught him, and cast him out of the vineyard, and slew him. When the lord therefore of the vineyard cometh, what will he do unto those husbandmen?"

They say unto **Him**, "He will miserably destroy those wicked men, and will let out his vineyard unto other husbandmen, which shall render him the fruits in their seasons."

And the **Boy** saith unto them, **"Did ye never read in**

the scriptures, 'The stone which the builders rejected, the same is become the head of the corner: this is the LORD's doing, and it is marvellous in our eyes?'

"Therefore say I unto you, 'The kingdom of God shall be taken from you, and given to a nation bringing forth the fruits thereof. And whosoever shall fall on this stone shall be broken: but on whomsoever it shall fall, it will grind him to powder.' "

And when the chief priests and Pharisees had heard **His** nursery story, they perceived that **He** spake of them. But when they sought to lay hands on **Him**, they feared the multitude, because they took **Him** for a mere **Boy**.

With outrage and full of wrath, Caiaphas raised the back of his hand to strike the **Boy** on his right cheek and the **Boy** did not wince. Remembering the words of the **Boy**, Caiaphas caught his hand in shame, but then, seething with the heat of anger, ordered the Temple guards to remove forcibly the **Boy** from the Temple of Solomon King and return only once **He** was older and more learned in the ways and means of the Law of Moses Lawgiver as the elders and the chief priests and the scribes perceived it: not as the **LORD** their **God** breathed the Law into Moses' mouth and written by Moses' pen, but as mere elders and mere chief priests and mere scribes chose to interpret the **Word of God**, rejecting the understanding of the **Word of God by** The Word!

"The journey of our allotted life, for the LORD hath given the days of our years at threescore years and ten; and if by reason of strength they be fourscore years, yet is our strength labour and sorrow; for it is soon cut off, and we fly away. I am allotted a mere half of yours. In a mere score of years, I must suffer many things, and be rejected

He, *as a mere boy, argues the scriptures whilst about* His *Father's business.*

of ye, the elders and chief priests and scribes, and be slain, and be raised the third day." The Boy, then, walked over to a cage of doves and released the doves into the air with great fanfare.

The Boy's parents journey from their hamlet in the Galilee to Jerusalem every year at the Feats of Passover. And when they had fulfilled the days, as they returned, the Boy tarried behind in Jerusalem; and Joseph of Nazareth and His Mother Mary, knew not. But they, supposing Him to have been in the caravan, went a day's journey, and they sought Him amongst their kinsfolk and acquaintances. And it came to pass, that after three days, returning to Jerusalem alone and at risk from highwaymen, and searching though the whole of the Holy City, they found Him in there releasing doves into the air. His mother said unto Him, "Son, why has Thou thus dealt with us. Behold Thy father and I have sought Thee sorrowing?"

And the Boy said unto them, "How is it that you sought Me? Did you not know that I must be in My Father's House and be about My Father's business."

Chapter 1
"Vipers in the Bulrushes"

ORASMUCH MANY HAVE TAK-en in hand to watch the purported Messiah, **Jesus, the son of Joseph of Nazareth of the Galilee**, whether it be the courtiers and sol-diers of Herod Antipas leery of usurpers, the Romans wary of insurrectionaries, or the Sanhedrin ever weary of the mo-notonous rise of endless Messiahs. The Sanhedrin sent forth spies, that I should feign myself **His** disciple, that I might take hold of **His** words and **His** deeds, which from the very beginning of **His** ministry reeked of blasphemy, witnessed by and influencing many into rebuking our authority, and sowing dissension amongst the multitudes against us and thereby reporting **His** words and **His** deeds to you, most ex-alted Caiaphas, that you might deliver **Him** unto the power and authority of the governor, Pontius Pilate.

Now being the fifteenth year of the reign of Tiberius

Caesar, Pontius Pilate being governor of Judaea, and Herod Antipas being tetrarch of Galilee and Perea, and his brother Philip tetrarch of Ituraea and of the region of Trachonitis, and Lysanias the tetrarch of Abilene, Annas and Caiaphas being the high priests, the word of God came unto John, the son of Zechariah in the wilderness.

John did baptize in the wilderness, and preach the baptism of repentance for the remission of sins. There went out unto him all the land of Judaea, and they of Jerusalem, and were all baptized of him in the river of Jordan, confessing their sins. And John was clothed with camel's hair, and with a girdle of a skin about his loins; and he did eat locusts and wild honey like a madman.

And I and my own brethren having been sent by the elders and chief priests and Levites from the Holy City's affluence into the wilderness to ask him, "Who art thou?" And he confessed, and denied not; but confessed, "I am not the **Christ**."

And we asked him, "What then? Art thou Elijah?" For we knoweth the Prophets and the warning of Malachi Messenger, 'Behold, **I** will send you Elijah Bodily Risen before the coming of the great and dreadful day of the **LORD**. And he shall turn the heart of the fathers to the children, and the heart of the children to their fathers, lest I come and smite the earth with a curse.' And yet John saith, "I am not." "Art thou that prophet?" And he again answered, "No."

Then said we unto him, "Who art thou? that we may give an answer to them that sent us. What sayest thou of thyself?" John said, "'**Comfort ye, comfort ye my people**,' saith your God. '**Speak ye comfortably to Jerusalem, and cry unto her, that her warfare is accomplished, that her iniquity is pardoned: for she hath received of the LORD's hand double for all her sins.**' "

Which answereth not our questions posed, and then John saith, seemingly aware of our consternation, "I am the voice of him that crieth in the wilderness, 'Prepare ye the way of the **LORD**, make straight in the desert a highway for our **God**. Every valley shall be exalted, and every mountain and hill shall be made low: and the crooked shall be made straight, and the rough places plain: And the glory of the **LORD** shall be revealed, and all flesh shall see it together: for the mouth of the **LORD** hath spoken it.

"The voice said, 'Cry! and 'What shall I cry?' All flesh is grass, and all the goodliness thereof is as the flower of the field: The grass withereth, the flower fadeth: because the spirit of the **LORD** bloweth upon it: surely the people is grass. The grass withereth, the flower fadeth: but the word of our **God** shall stand for ever.'

"O! Zion, that bringest good tidings, get thee up into the high mountain; O! Jerusalem, that bringest good tidings, lift up thy voice with strength; lift it up, be not afraid; say unto the cities of Judah, 'Behold your **God**!'

"Behold, the **LORD God** will come with strong hand, and **His** arm shall rule for him: behold, **His** reward is with **Him**, and **His** work before **Him**. **He** shall feed **His** flock like a shepherd: **He** shall gather the lambs with **His** arm, and carry them in **His** bosom, and shall gently lead those that are with young. Who hath measured the waters in the hollow of **His** hand, and meted out heaven with the span, and comprehended the dust of the earth in a measure, and weighed the mountains in scales, and the hills in a balance?

"Who hath directed the **Spirit** of the **LORD**, or being **His** counsellor hath taught **Him**? With whom took **He** counsel, and who instructed **Him**, and taught **Him** in the path of judgment, and taught **Him** knowledge, and shewed to **Him** the way of understanding? Behold, the nations are as a drop of a bucket, and are counted as the small dust of the balance: behold, **He** taketh up the isles as a very little thing. And Lebanon is not sufficient to burn, nor the beasts thereof sufficient for a burnt offering. All nations before **Him** are as nothing; and they are counted to **Him** less than nothing, and vanity.

"To whom then will ye liken **God**? or what likeness will ye compare unto **Him**? The workman melteth a graven image, and the goldsmith spreadeth it over with gold, and casteth silver chains. He that is so impoverished that he hath no oblation chooseth a tree that will not rot; he seeketh unto him a cunning workman to prepare a graven image, that shall not be moved.

"Have ye not known? have ye not heard? hath it not been told you from the beginning? have ye not understood from the foundations of the earth? It is **He** that sitteth upon the circle of the earth, and the inhabitants thereof are as grasshoppers; that stretcheth out the heavens as a curtain, and spreadeth them out as a tent to dwell in: that bringeth the princes to nothing; **He** maketh the judges of the earth as vanity.

"Yea, they shall not be planted; yea, they shall not be sown: yea, their stock shall not take root in the earth: and he shall also blow upon them, and they shall wither, and the whirlwind shall take them away as stubble.

" '**To whom then will ye liken Me, or shall I be equal?**' saith the **Holy One**. Lift up your eyes on high, and behold who hath created these things, that bringeth out their host by number: **He** calleth them all by names by the greatness of his might, for that he is strong in power; not one faileth.

"Why sayest thou, O! Jacob, and speakest, O! Israel,

'My way is hid from the **LORD**, and my judgment is passed over from my **God**?' Hast thou not known? hast thou not heard, that the everlasting **God**, **the LORD**, **the Creator** of the ends of the earth, fainteth not, neither is weary? there is no searching of his understanding. **He** giveth power to the faint; and to them that have no might **He** increaseth strength. Even the youths shall faint and be weary, and the young men shall utterly fall: But they that wait upon the **LORD** shall renew their strength; they shall mount up with wings as eagles; they shall run, and not be weary; and they shall walk, and not faint, as saith the prophet Isaiah."

And we which were sent were of the Pharisees. And we asked him, and said unto him, "Why baptizest thou then, if thou be not that **Christ**, nor Elijah, neither that prophet?" John answered us, saying, "I indeed baptize with water unto repentance: but **He** that cometh after me is mightier than I and **He** standeth one among you, whom ye know not; **He** it is, who coming after me is preferred before me, whose shoe's latchet I am not worthy to unloose."

Then said he to the multitude that came forth to be baptized of him, "O! generation of vipers, who hath warned you to flee from the wrath to come? Bring forth therefore fruits worthy of repentance, and begin not to say within yourselves, 'We have Abraham to our father': for I say unto you that **God** is able of these stones to raise up children unto Abraham."

Fie! Out upon the Baptizer! How dare he call us vipers slithering amongst the bulrushes cursed above all cattle, and above every beast of the field; upon our belly shalt we go, and dust shalt we eat all the days of our life!

Have faith my brethren! John, and those like whom John prophesies whose shoe's latchet he is not worthy to unloose, only presume they knoweth knowledge that we are hypocrites! for we shut up the kingdom of heaven against men: for we neither go in yourselves, neither suffer we them that are entering to go in; we devour widows' houses, and for a pretence make long prayer: therefore ye shall receive the greater damnation; we compass sea and land to make one proselyte, and when he is made, we make him twofold more the child of hell than ourselves.

We blind guides, which say, "Whosoever shall swear by the temple, it is nothing; but whosoever shall swear by the gold of the temple, he is a debtor!" Art we fools and blind: for whether is greater, the gold, or the temple that sanctifieth the gold? And we further say, foolishly and blindly "Whosoever shall swear by the altar, it is nothing; but whosoever sweareth by the gift that is upon it, he is guilty." Art we fools and blind: for whether is greater, the gift, or the altar that sanctifieth the gift? For whom says "Therefore shall swear by the altar, sweareth by it, and by all things thereon. And whoso shall swear by the temple, sweareth by it, and by him that dwelleth therein. And he that shall swear by heaven, sweareth by the throne of God, and by him that sitteth thereon"? A fool that is whom!

We are hypocrites! for we pay tithe of mint and anise and cummin, and have omitted the weightier matters of the law, judgment, mercy, and faith: these ought ye to have done, and not to leave the other undone. We blind guides, which strain at a gnat, and swallow a camel. We make clean the outside of the cup and of the platter, but within they are full of extortion and excess; we cleanse first that which is within the cup and platter, that the outside of them may be clean also. We are like unto whited sepulchres, which indeed appear beautiful outward, but are within full of dead men's bones, and of all uncleanness. Even so we also outwardly appear righteous unto men, but within ye are full of hypocrisy and iniquity. We build the tombs of the prophets, and garnish the sepulchres of the righteous, And say, "If we had been in the days of our fathers, we would not have been partakers with them in the blood of the prophets." Wherefore we be witnesses unto ourselves, that we are the children of them which killed the prophets. Fill we up then the measure of our fathers.

Wherefore, behold, if the LORD God send unto us prophets, and wise men, and scribes: and some of them we shall kill and crucify; and some of them shall we scourge in our synagogues, and persecute them from city to city: that upon you may come all the righteous blood shed upon the earth, from the blood of righteous Abel unto the blood of Zacharias son of Barachias, whom we slew between the temple and the altar.

Shall all these things shall come upon this generation? Fie! Out upon the Baptizer! We, the elders and the chief priests and the scribes, killest the prophets, and stonest them which are sent unto us, how often would the LORD have gathered her children together, even as a hen gathereth her chickens under her wings, and we would not!

These enigmatic and problematic Messianic and threatful activities of the Baptizer in the wilderness is anathema to the influence and affluence of God we alone wield. And! must we cometh from the comforts and qualities our palaces to the wilderness of the river Jordan to inquire upon the revolutionary activities of the fraudulent prophet, whose very testimonies undermine the authority of the elders and the chief priests and the scribes! The LORD God of Israel hath commanded us to maketh blood sacrifices and burnt offerings in the Temple of Solomon rebuilt by the great Herod King for the absolution of sins. Who is he to free the people of their sins? And who is he to cast them into the fire? With water!

The Baptizer mayest deny being Isaiah, but doth he claim to be Ezekiel? For John saith unto the multitudes, "The LORD God saith, 'When I shall be sanctified in you before their eyes. For I will take you from among the heathen, and gather you out of all countries, and will bring you into your own land. Then will I sprinkle clean water upon you, and ye shall be clean: from all your filthiness, and from all your idols, will I cleanse you. A new heart also will I give you, and a new spirit will I put within you: and I will take away the stony heart out of your flesh, and I will give you an heart of flesh. And I will put My spirit within you, and cause you to walk in my statutes, and ye shall keep My judgments, and do them. And ye shall dwell in the land that I gave to your fathers; and ye shall be my people, and I will be your God. I will also save you from all your uncleannesses: and I will call for the corn, and will increase it, and lay no famine upon you. And I will multiply the fruit of the tree, and the increase of the field, that ye shall receive no more reproach of famine among the heathen. Then shall ye remember your own evil ways, and your doings that were not good, and shall lothe yourselves in your own sight for your iniquities and for your abominations. Not for your sakes do I this,' saith the Lord God, 'be it known unto you: be ashamed and confounded for your own ways, O! house of Israel.'

"And now also the axe is laid unto the root of the trees: every tree therefore which bringeth not forth good fruit is hewn down, and cast into the fire."

And the people asked him, saying, "What shall we do then?" He answereth and saith unto them as if he has authority, "He that hath two coats, let him impart to him that hath none; and he that hath meat, let him do likewise."

Then came also publicans to be baptized, and said unto him, "Master, what shall we do?" And he said unto them, "Exact no more than that which is appointed you."

And the soldiers likewise demanded of him, saying, "And what shall we do?" And he said unto them, "Do violence to no man, neither accuse any falsely; and be content with your wages."

And as the people were in expectation, and all men mused in their hearts of John, whether he were the **Christ**, or not; John answered, saying unto them all, "I indeed baptize you with water; but one mightier than I cometh, the latchet of whose shoes I am not worthy to unloose: **He** shall baptize you with the **Holy Ghost** and with fire: **Whose** fan is in **His** hand, and **He** will thoroughly purge **His** floor, and will gather the wheat into **His** garner; but the chaff **He** will burn with fire unquenchable. And many other things in his exhortation preached **He** unto the people."

These things were done in Bethabara beyond Jordan, where John was baptizing. The next day John seeth a Nazarene coming unto him, and saith, "Behold the **Lamb of God**, which taketh away the sin of the world." Doth John warn us Isaiah's suffering servant? What have we to fear of **Him**? **He** shalt be oppressed and afflicted, yet **He** opens not **His** mouth: **He** is brought as a lamb to slaughter, and as a sheep for her shearers is dumb, so **He** openeth not his mouth. We possess no fear not this **Lamb**. And John continueth, "This is **He** of whom I said, after me cometh a **Man** which is preferred before me: for **He** was before me.

And I knew **Him** not: but that **He** should be made manifest to Israel, therefore am I come baptizing with water."

    And as I bare this record unto thee most exalted Caiaphas that the Baptist saith, "I saw the **Spirit** descending from **heaven** like a dove, and it abode upon **Him**. And I knew **Him** not: but **He** that sent me to baptize with water, the same said unto me, '**Upon whom thou shalt see the Spirit descending, and remaining on him, the same is He which baptizeth with the Holy Ghost,**' as if to saith, '**Why do the heathen rage, and the people imagine a vain thing? The kings of the earth set themselves, and the rulers take counsel together, against the LORD, and against His Anointed, saying, "Let us break their bands asunder, and cast away their cords from us." He that sitteth in the heavens shall laugh: the LORD shall have them in derision. Then shall He speak unto them in His wrath, and vex them in His sore displeasure. Yet have I set My king upon My holy hill of Zion. I will declare the decree: the LORD hath said unto Him, "Thou art My Son; this day have I begotten Thee. Ask of Me, and I shall give Thee the heathen for Thine inheritance, and the uttermost parts of the earth for Thy possession. Thou shalt break them with a rod of iron; thou shalt dash them in pieces like a potter's vessel." Be wise now therefore, O! ye kings: be instructed, ye judges of the earth. Serve the Lord with fear, and rejoice with trembling. Kiss the Son, lest He**

The baptism of Jesus while the vipers watch from the bulrushes.

be angry, and ye perish from the way, when His wrath is kindled but a little. Blessed are all they that put their trust in Him.' " And John saw, and bare record that this is the **Son of God**.

We, as the council of the Sanhedrin sitting together, siaith "What do we? for John claimeth this **Man** is the Messiah. If we let **Him** thus alone, all men will believe on **Him**: and the Romans shall come and take away both our place and nation." And one of us, named Caiaphas, being the high priest that same year, said unto us, "Ye know nothing at all, nor consider that it is expedient for us, that one man should die for the people, and that the whole nation perish not. And this spake he not of himself: but being high priest that year, he prophesied that **He** should die for that nation; And not for that nation only, but that also he should gather together in one the children of **God** that were scattered abroad."

And was put for as my task to watch **Him**, and feign myself as a sycophant of the **false Messiah**, that I might take hold of **His** words, that so that we might deliver **Him** unto the power and authority of the governor of Judaea, Pontius Pilate. As the elders and the chief priests and the scribes, we know the knowledge of the vindictiveness and furious temper of the governor, who is naturally inflexible, a blend of self-will and relentlessness and his corruption, and his acts of insolence, and his rapine, and his habit of insulting people, and his cruelty, and his continual murders of people untried and uncondemned, and his never ending, and gratuitous, and most grievous inhumanity[1] that he alone might silence this self-styled **Messiah**, this purported and preposterous **Son of God**! ✝

---
1 Philo, *On The Embassy of Gauis* Book XXXVIII

Chapter 2
"The Scourging of the Temple"

UR PASSOVER WAS AT HAND that we shouldst observe the month of Abib, and keep the passover unto the **LORD** our **God**: for in the month of Abib the **LORD** thy **God** brought us forth out of Egypt by night. This nascent Messiah three times in a year must appear before the **LORD His God**: the feast of unleavened bread, and in the feast of weeks, and in the feast of tabernacles, and **He** shall not appear before the **LORD** empty for every man shall give as **He** is able, according to the blessing of the **LORD thy God** which **He** hath given unto **Him**. And how doth this inchoate Messiah return the blessings given by **His LORD**?

The elders and the chief priests and the scribes of the Holy City witnessed and reported unto Caiaphas, the High-Priest, and to the Sanhedrin the crimes and the heresies of **Jesus of Nazareth of the Galilee**. **He** found in the our great

Temple within the Court of Gentiles those permitted to sell oxen and sheep and doves, and those that sold souvenirs to travellers from on far, and the changers of money sitting. He believeth He is the fulfilment of Ezekiel Captive of Babylon who as the holy flock, as the flock of Jerusalem in her solemn feasts; so shall the waste cities be filled with flocks of men: and they shall know that He is the LORD.

When He had made a scourge of small cords, He drove them all out of the Temple full of the wrath and violence of a raver or revolutionary; and the sheep, and the oxen were not spared His anger nor the scourging of His cord, their bleating cried throughout the Temple as they trampled innocents, breaking bones and cracking skulls, as they sought their escape; and He poured out the changers' money scattering the shekels upon the stones, and overthrew the tables in a tantrum. His scourge striped the money-changers and those that sold souvenirs to travellers and doves for burnt offerings. The whip of cords split the skin of the peddlers unloosing a veritable flood of blood from their brows and cheeks so that they shrieked and wailed from the assail, fleeing amidst their pleading. And He said unto them sanctioned to sell their wares within the court, "Take these things hence; make not My Father's house an house of merchandise."

As though we were covetous and avaricious priests desirous more of silver and gold than the will and worship of the LORD! Did not David King buy the offerings of Araunah at a price: neither would he offer burnt offerings unto the LORD his God what belongs of Araunah or offer burnt offerings which doth cost him nothing? So David bought the threshingfloor and the oxen for fifty shekels of silver. We

He chases the money-changers from the house of merchandise— nay, His Father's house!

maketh not the house of the **LORD** into a bazaar!

And then **He** saith, cavorting and raving madly in the drunkenness of **His** zeal, "O! God, thou knowest **My** foolishness; and My sins are not hid from Thee. Let not them that wait on Thee, O! LORD God of hosts, be ashamed for My sake: let not those that seek Thee be confounded for My sake, O! God of Israel. Because for Thy sake I have borne reproach; shame hath covered My face. I am become a stranger unto My brethren, and an alien unto My mother's children. For the zeal of Thine house hath eaten Me up; and the reproaches of them that reproached thee are fallen upon Me. When I wept, and chastened My soul with fasting, that was to My reproach. I made sackcloth also My garment; and I became a proverb to them. They that sit in the gate speak against Me; and I was the song of the drunkards." Knoweth we did what **He** desireth us to hear is in **His** words: "For the zeal of **Thine** house hath eaten **Me** up."

Then answered our fellows did and said unto **Him**, "What sign shewest **Thou** unto us, seeing that **Thou** doest these things?" We believeth not in **Him** until like Aaron **He** taketh **His** scourge of cords and cast if before us and it becometh a serpent.

Howbeit, **He** answered and said unto our fellows, **"Destroy this temple, and in three days I will raise it up."** Then the Jews mockingly guffawed and saith, "Forty and six years was this temple in building, and wilt **Thou** rear it up in three days?" We rightfully and righteously rebuked the ramblings of this raving revolutionary.

Three days? Three days! Fie!

The **LORD God of Israel** alone knoweth the means of men to destroy **His** great work! when it came to pass in the ninth year of his reign, in the tenth month, in the

tenth day of the month, that Nebuchadnezzar king of Babylon came, he, and all his host, against Jerusalem, and pitched against it; and they built forts against it round about. And the city was besieged. And in the fifth month, on the seventh day of the month, which is the nineteenth year of king Nebuchadnezzar king of Babylon, came Nebuzaradan, captain of the guard, a servant of the king of Babylon, unto Jerusalem: and he burnt the house of the LORD, and the king's house, and all the houses of Jerusalem, and every great man's house burnt he with fire. And all the army of the Chaldees, that were with the captain of the guard, brake down the walls of Jerusalem round about. And the pillars of brass that were in the house of the LORD, and the bases, and the brasen sea that was in the house of the LORD, did the Chaldees break in pieces, and carried the brass of them to Babylon. And the pots, and the shovels, and the snuffers, and the spoons, and all the vessels of brass wherewith they ministered, took they away. And the firepans, and the bowls, and such things as were of gold, in gold, and of silver, in silver, the captain of the guard took away and Judah was in the same wise taken away out of their land for a score and twenty years.

And to raise the Temple in three days what taketh armies of men to raze in five months! Fie! Out upon **Jesus of Nazareth of the Galilee! His** madness shalt prove infectious! The commission to raise the Temple was for Cyrus king of Persia and Herod king of Judea and not **Jesus**, the carpenter's son.

The prophet Ezra knoweth Cyrus King saith, "The **LORD God of heaven** hath given me all the kingdoms of the earth; and **He** hath charged me to build him an house at Jerusalem, which is in Judah. Who is there among you

The Hebrew are taken into Babylonian captivity!

of all his people? his **God** be with him, and let him go up to Jerusalem, which is in Judah, and build the house of the **LORD God of Israel**, **He** is the **God**,) which is in Jerusalem. And whosoever remaineth in any place where he sojourneth, let the men of his place help him with silver, and with gold, and with goods, and with beasts, beside the freewill offering for the house of **God** that is in Jerusalem"

And for Great Herod King who undertook a very great work; that is to build of himself the temple of **God**, and make it larger in compass, and to raise it to a most magnificent altitude: as esteeming it to be the most glorious of all his actions, as it really was, to bring it to perfection; and that this would be sufficient for an everlasting memorial of him. But as he knew the multitude were not ready nor willing to assist him in so vast a design; he thought to prepare them first by making a speech to them; and then to set about the work itself. So he called them together, and spake thus to them: "I think I need not speak to you, my countrymen, about such other works as I have done, since I came to the Kingdom: although I may say they have been performed in such a manner as to bring more security to you, than glory to my self. For I have neither been negligent in the most difficult times about what tended to ease your necessities: nor have the buildings I have made been so proper to preserve me, as yourselves from injuries. And I imagine that, with **God's** assistance, I have advanced the nation of the Jews to a degree of happiness which they never had before. And for the particular edifices belonging to your own country, and your own cities; as also to those cities that we have lately acquired, which we have erected, and greatly adorned, and thereby augmented the dignity of your nation; it seems to me a needless task to enumerate them to you: since you well know them yourselves. But as to that undertaking which I have a mind to set about at present, and which will be a work of the greatest piety and excellence that can possibly be undertaken by us; I will now declare it to you. Our Fathers indeed, when they were returned from Babylon, built this temple to **God Almighty**. Yet does it want sixty cubits of its largeness in altitude. For so much did that first temple which Solomon built exceed this temple. Nor let any one condemn our fathers for their negligence or want of piety herein. For it was not their fault, that the temple was no higher. For they were Cyrus, and Darius the son of Hystaspes, who determined the measures for its rebuilding. And it hath been by reason of the subjection of those fathers of ours to them and to their posterity, and after them to the Macedonians, that they had not the opportunity to follow the original model of this pious edifice; nor could raise it to its ancient altitude. But since I am now, by **God's** will, your Governor; and I have had peace a long time, and have gained great riches, and large revenues; and, what is the principal thing of all, I am in amity with and well regarded by the Romans; who, if I may so say, are the rulers of the whole world; I will do my endeavour to correct that imperfection, which hath arisen from the necessity of our affairs, and the slavery we have been under formerly: and to make a thankful return, after the most pious manner, to **God**, for what blessings I have received from **Him**, by giving me this Kingdom, and that by rendering **His** temple as complete as I am able."[1]

And Herod the king by the will of his authority raised the Temple in six and forty years. Fie! upon this revolutionary armed with scourge made of small cords to believe **He** could raze the Temple to the ground and in three days raise

---

[1] Josephus, *Antiquites of the Jews* Book XV Chapter 11.1

the Temple from the ground! Doth **He** speak in metaphors **His** own idled and mad mind comprehendeth? Doth **He** spake of the temple of **His** body? Doth **His** disciples seek to rob **His** unavoidable grave of **His** body upon the third day so that these words suggest **He** is risen? Absurdities laid on the foundation of madness! ✠

Chapter 3
"Rejected at Nazareth"

VER THY FAITHFUL SERVANT, journey did I in a return to the backwater of the Galilee, to shadow this rumored and infant **Messiah** in the caravan that traveled north towards the direction of Sepphoris. **He** left the caravan at a hamlet not-a-thing good can come out of known as Nazareth, where **He** had been reared as the son of Joseph of Nazareth, born unto the city of David, which is called Bethlehem (because he was of the house and linage of David). Fair forewarning must be addressed of the Words the **LORD God of Israel** saith unto David King:

"And when thy days be fulfilled, and thou shalt sleep with thy fathers, I will set up thy seed after thee, which shall proceed out of thy bowels, and I will establish His kingdom. He shall build an house for My name, and I will stablish the throne of His kingdom for ever. I will be

His father, and He shall be My son. If he commit iniquity, I will chasten Him with the rod of men, and with the stripes of the children of men: But my mercy shall not depart away from Him, as I took it from Saul, whom I put away before thee. And thine house and thy kingdom shall be established for ever before thee: thy throne shall be established for ever."

And this is worrisome for the plentiful purported Messiahs know of the knowledge of the prophesies the **LORD God of Israel** breathed into our most sacred of scriptures, not only of the books of most esteemed of Prophets but throughout its entire Word; and these shamful Messiahs attempteth to shoehorn their lives and their deeds to those of the one true Messiah. A portion of the prophecies foretelling the Messiah are not in the control of this minor **Messiah** (by its very nature the lineage of his birth), but many of the multitudes art surely manipulated by a Messiah armed with the knowledge found in our most sacred of scriptures, the very prophesies the **LORD God of Israel** hath breathed. The prophecies are not the secret knowledge mystery cults for the eyes and ears of the membership. The **LORD God of Israel** skulks not in the shadows of a torch filled night or the depths of caves and catacombs, but proclaims his prophecies to the entirety of **His** Chosen People: the whole of the land of Israel. Our minds and our faith shalt not be clouded so easily as the common folk when this **Jesus of Nazareth of the Galilee** proclaimeth **He** fulfills and is the fulfillment of the very breathe of the **LORD God of Israel**. Must we be prepared to rebuke the fulfillments of prophecy as they arise, and they shalt, for this is but the first of scores this purported Messiah shalt claim— this very day.

He returned in the power of the **Spirit** into Galilee: and there went out a fame of **Him** through all the region round about. And **He** taught in their synagogues, being glorified of all. And, as **His** custom was, **He** went into the synagogue on the sabbath day, and stood up for to read. And there was delivered unto **Him** the book of the prophet Isaiah. And when **He** had opened the book, **He** found the place where it was written:

"The Spirit of the Lord God is upon Me; because the LORD hath anointed Me to preach good tidings unto the meek; He hath sent Me to bind up the broken-hearted, to proclaim liberty to the captives, and the opening of the prison to them that are bound; to proclaim the acceptable year of the LORD, and the day of vengeance of our God; to comfort all that mourn; to appoint unto them that mourn in Zion, to give unto them beauty for ashes, the oil of joy for mourning, the garment of praise for the spirit of heaviness; that they might be called trees of righteousness, the planting of the LORD, that he might be glorified.

"And they shall build the old wastes, they shall raise up the former desolations, and they shall repair the waste cities, the desolations of many generations. And strangers shall stand and feed your flocks, and the sons of the alien shall be your plowmen and your vinedressers. But ye shall be named the Priests of the LORD: men shall call you the Ministers of our God: ye shall eat the riches of the Gentiles, and in their glory shall ye boast yourselves. For your shame ye shall have double; and for confusion they shall rejoice in their portion: therefore in their land they shall possess the double: everlasting joy shall be unto them.

"For I the Lord love judgment, I hate robbery for burnt offering; and I will direct their work in truth, and I

He teaches in the synagogue at Nazareth and the Pharisees are not agog at His blasphemy!

will make an everlasting covenant with them. And their seed shall be known among the Gentiles, and their offspring among the people: all that see them shall acknowledge them, that they are the seed which the LORD hath blessed.

"I will greatly rejoice in the LORD, My soul shall be joyful in My God; for He hath clothed Me with the garments of salvation, He hath covered Me with the robe of righteousness, as a bridegroom decketh himself with ornaments, and as a bride adorneth herself with her jewels. For as the earth bringeth forth her bud, and as the garden causeth the things that are sown in it to spring forth; so the LORD God will cause righteousness and praise to spring forth before all the nations."

And He closed the book, and He gave it again to the minister, and sat down. And the eyes of all them that were in the synagogue were fastened on Him. And He began to say unto them, "This day is this scripture fulfilled in your ears." And all bare Him witness, and wondered at the gracious words which proceeded out of His mouth. Some saith, "Thou art fairer than the children of men: grace is poured into Thy lips: therefore God hath blessed Thee for ever." But more said, "Is not this Joseph's son?"

And He said unto them, "Ye will surely say unto Me this proverb, 'Physician, heal thyself: whatsoever we have heard done in Capernaum, do also here in thy country'" And He said, "Verily I say unto you, 'No prophet is accepted in his own country.' But I tell you of a truth, many widows were in Israel in the days of Elias, when the heaven was shut up three years and six months, when great famine was throughout all the land; but unto none of them was Elias sent, save unto Sarepta, a city of Sidon, unto a woman that was a widow. And many lepers were in Israel in the time of Eliseus the prophet; and none of them was cleansed, saving Naaman the Syrian."

And all they in the synagogue, the elders and the chief priests and the scribes and the men when they heard these things, were filled with wrath, and rose up, and buffeted **Him** with their hands and the backs of their hands, and they made a scourge of small cords and drove **Him** out of the synagogue into the street, saying in unison, "Knoweth the knowledge of our most sacred of scriptures, but knoweth this knowledge: "There riseth up among you a **prophet**, or a **dreamer of dreams**, and giveth thee a sign or a wonder, and the sign or the wonder come to pass, whereof **He** spake unto thee, saying, '**Let us go after other gods, which thou hast not known, and let us serve them**'; thou shalt not hearken unto the words of that **prophet**, or that **dreamer of dreams**: for the **LORD** your **God** proveth you, to know whether ye love the **LORD** your **God** with all your heart and with all your soul. Ye shall walk after the **LORD** your **God**, and fear **Him**, and keep **His** commandments, and obey **His** voice, and ye shall serve **Him**, and cleave unto **Him**. And that **prophet**, or that **dreamer of dreams**, shall be put to death; because **He** hath spoken to turn you away from the **LORD** your **God**, which brought you out of the land of Egypt, and redeemed you out of the house of bondage, to thrust thee out of the way which the **LORD** thy **God** commanded thee to walk in. So shalt thou put the evil away from the midst of thee.

"If thy brother, the son of thy mother, or thy son, or

thy daughter, or the wife of thy bosom, or thy friend, which is as thine own soul, entice thee secretly, saying, 'Let us go and serve other gods', which thou hast not known, thou, nor thy fathers; namely, of the gods of the people which are round about you, nigh unto thee, or far off from thee, from the one end of the earth even unto the other end of the earth; thou shalt not consent unto **Him**, nor hearken unto **Him**; neither shall thine eye pity **Him**, neither shalt thou spare, neither shalt thou conceal **Him**: But thou shalt surely kill **Him**; thine hand shall be first upon **Him** to put **Him** to death, and afterwards the hand of all the people."

And the Nazarenes thrust **Him** out of the city, and led **Him** unto the brow of the hill whereon their city was built, that they might cast **Him** down headlong onto the rocks below, breaking his bones and the bones of his skull on the jagged refuse of rubble. But **He** passing through the midst of us unseen went upon **His** way. Is **He** a sorcerer who causeth children to pass through the fire in the valley of the son of Hinnom? Also has **He** observed times, and used enchantments, and used witchcraft, and dealt with a familiar spirit, and with wizards? Has **He** wrought much evil in the sight of the **LORD**, to provoke **Him** to anger? Nay! Faith! **He** is but in the likeness of a court conjurer of parlor tricks that delight the idle minds of aristocrats and their sycophants, that causeth **Him** to pass through the midst of us unseen and goeth upon **His** way.

O! Caiaphas! Troubled am I not by **His** supposed sorcery but Lo! Woe! remembereth the prophecy of the Psalmist, "The stone which the builders refused is become the head stone of the corner. This is the **LORD's** doing; it is marvellous in our eyes. This is the day which the **LORD** hath made; we will rejoice and be glad in it." 'Tis but the second prophecy of the Christ this son of a carpenter hath fulfilled on this day. Must we be wary and watchful of **Jesus of Nazareth of the Galilee** or else all of our power and influence over the whole of Israel be lost.

And leaving Nazareth, **He** came and dwelt in Capernaum, which is upon the sea coast, in the borders of Zabulon and Nephthalim: That Lo! Woe! **His** knowledge of the scriptures is mysterious and great! So great, verily, that through **His** choice for the infancy of his ministry as **Messiah** it might be fulfilled which was spoken by Isaiah the prophet, saying:

"Nevertheless the dimness shall not be such as was in her vexation, when at the first he lightly afflicted the land of Zebulun and the land of Naphtali, and afterward did more grievously afflict her by the way of the sea, beyond Jordan, in Galilee of the nations. The people that walked in darkness have seen a great light: they that dwell in the land of the shadow of death, upon them hath the light sprung up. **Thou** hast multiplied the nation, and not increased the joy: they joy before thee according to the joy in harvest, and as men rejoice when they divide the spoil. For **Thou** hast broken the yoke of his burden, and the staff of his shoulder, the rod of his oppressor, as in the day of Midian. For every battle of the warrior is with confused noise, and garments rolled in blood; but this shall be with burning and fuel of fire. For unto us a child is born, unto us a **Son** is given: and the government shall be upon **His** shoulder: and **His** name shall be called **Wonderful**, **Counsellor**, **The Mighty God**, **The Everlasting Father**, **The Prince of Peace**. Of the increase of **His** government and peace there shall be no end, upon the throne of David, and upon **His** kingdom, to order it, and to establish it with judgment and with justice from henceforth even for ever. The zeal of the Lord of hosts will perform this."

And it came to pass, that, as the people pressed upon him to hear the word of God, **He** stood by the lake of Gennesaret, and saw two ships standing by the lake: but the fishermen were gone out of them, and were washing their nets. And **He** entered into one of the ships, which was Simon's, and prayed him that he would thrust out a little from the land. And **He** sat down, and taught the people out of the ship.

Now when **He** had left speaking, **He** said unto Simon, **"Launch out into the deep, and let down your nets for a draught."**

And Simon answering said unto **Him**, "Master, we have toiled all the night, and have taken nothing: nevertheless at **Thy** word I will let down the net." And when they had this done, they inclosed a great multitude of fishes: and their net brake. And they beckoned unto their partners, which were in the other ship, that they should come and help them. And they came, and filled both the ships, so that they began to sink and water sheeted over the prow as the weight of the draught of fish sought to drawn them all. When Simon Peter saw it, he fell down at **His** knees, saying, "Depart from me; for I am a sinful man, O! **Lord**."

For Simon was astonished, and all that were with him, at the draught of the fishes which they had taken: and so was also James, and John, the sons of Zebedee, which were partners with Simon. And **He** said unto Simon, **"Fear not. Follow Me. And henceforth I will make you fishers of**

He *lures two fishermen from their livelihood to their eventual deaths by execution!*

men."

Who were these fishermen to be called upon to be Disciples of this **false Messiah**? The elders and the chief priests and the scribes of Nazareth rightfully and righteously rejecteth **His** teachings and **His** blasphemy, so turneth **He** does to the poorest of the poor, the lowliest of the low.

Fishers of men? Bah! It is a humbug!

Doth not Malachi saith of the Disciples of the True Messiah: "**Behold, I will send My messenger, and he shall prepare the way before Me: and the LORD, whom ye seek, shall suddenly come to His temple, even the messenger of the covenant, whom ye delight in: behold, He shall come. But who may abide the day of His coming? and who shall stand when he appeareth? for He is like a refiner's fire, and like fullers' soap: And He shall sit as a refiner and purifier of silver: And He shall purify the sons of Levi, and purge them as gold and silver, that they may offer unto the Lord an offering in righteousness**"?

These fishers of men are not of the priesthood of Levi!

Did not the **LORD God of Israel** saith unto Aaron: "**Thou and thy sons and thy father's house with thee shall bear the iniquity of the sanctuary: and thou and thy sons with thee shall bear the iniquity of your priesthood. And thy brethren also of the tribe of Levi, the tribe of thy father, bring thou with thee, that they may be joined unto thee, and minister unto thee: but thou and thy sons with thee shall minister before the tabernacle of witness. And they shall keep thy charge, and the charge of all the tabernacle: only they shall not come nigh the vessels of the sanctuary and the altar, that neither they, nor ye also, die. And they shall be joined unto thee, and keep the charge of the tabernacle of the congregation, for all the service** of the tabernacle: and a stranger shall not come nigh unto you. And ye shall keep the charge of the sanctuary, and the charge of the altar: that there be no wrath any more upon the children of Israel"?

And when these fishers of men had brought their ships to land, they forsook all, and followed **Him**— and follow **Him** I did, howbeit I forsook not my own teachings and teachers, for my task set by the Sanhedrin and the High Priest is to watch **Him** and to listen to **Him** and feign myself as a sycophant of this **false Messiah** as **His** trusted disciple, that I might take hold of **His** teachings, **His** words, these very words so that they mayest be a sword armed against **Him**.

The words of woe to foolish prophets as breathed from God through Ezekiel must I record here: "**Son of man, prophesy against the prophets of Israel that prophesy, and say thou unto them that prophesy out of their own hearts, 'Hear ye the word of the LORD!'** "

Thus saith the Lord God: "**Woe unto the foolish prophets, that follow their own spirit, and have seen nothing! O! Israel, thy prophets are like the foxes in the deserts. Ye have not gone up into the gaps, neither made up the hedge for the house of Israel to stand in the battle in the day of the Lord. They have seen vanity and lying divination, saying, 'The Lord saith': and the Lord hath not sent them: and they have made others to hope that they would confirm the word. Have ye not seen a vain vision, and have ye not spoken a lying divination, whereas ye say, 'The Lord saith it'; albeit I have not spoken?**

"Because ye have spoken vanity, and seen lies, therefore, behold, I am against you, and mine hand shall be upon the prophets that see vanity, and that divine lies: they shall not be in the assembly of my people, neither shall they be written in the writing of the house of Israel, neither shall they enter into the land of Israel; and ye shall know that I am the LORD God."

Thus the Lord God saith: "Because, even because they have seduced My people, saying, 'Peace'; and there was no peace; and one built up a wall, and, lo, others daubed it with untempered morter: Say unto them which daub it with untempered morter, that it shall fall: there shall be an overflowing shower; and ye, O! great hailstones, shall fall; and a stormy wind shall rend it. Lo, when the wall is fallen, shall it not be said unto you, 'Where is the daubing wherewith ye have daubed it?' "

Thus the Lord God saith: "I will even rend it with a stormy wind in my fury; and there shall be an overflowing shower in mine anger, and great hailstones in my fury to consume it. So will I break down the wall that ye have daubed with untempered morter, and bring it down to the ground, so that the foundation thereof shall be discovered, and it shall fall, and ye shall be consumed in the midst thereof: and ye shall know that I am the LORD.

"Thus will I accomplish My wrath upon the wall, and upon them that have daubed it with untempered morter, and will say unto you, 'The wall is no more, neither they that daubed it; to wit, the prophets of Israel which prophesy concerning Jerusalem, and which see visions of peace for her, and there is no peace.'

"Likewise, Thou Son of man, set Thy face against the daughters of thy people, which prophesy out of their own heart; and prophesy Thou against them, and say, 'Thus saith the Lord God; "Woe to the women that sew pillows to all armholes, and make kerchiefs upon the head of every stature to hunt souls! Will ye hunt the souls of my people, and will ye save the souls alive that come unto you? And will ye pollute Me among My people for handfuls of barley and for pieces of bread, to slay the souls that should not die, and to save the souls alive that should not live, by your lying to my people that hear your lies?" ' "

Wherefore thus saith the Lord God: "Behold, I am against your pillows, wherewith ye there hunt the souls to make them fly, and I will tear them from your arms, and will let the souls go, even the souls that ye hunt to make them fly. Your kerchiefs also will I tear, and deliver My people out of your hand, and they shall be no more in your hand to be hunted; and ye shall know that I am the LORD.

"Because with lies ye have made the heart of the righteous sad, whom I have not made sad; and strengthened the hands of the wicked, that he should not return from his wicked way, by promising him life: Therefore ye shall see no more vanity, nor divine divinations: for I will deliver my people out of your hand: and ye shall know that I am the LORD."

Chapter 4
"The Sorcery of Healing"

 ROM OUT OF THE SYNAGOGUE, they entered into the house of Simon and Andrew, with James and John. But Simon's wife's mother lay sick of a fever, and anon they tell him of her. And **He** came and took her by the hand, and lifted her up; and immediately the fever left her, and she ministered unto them. And at even, when the sun did set, they brought unto **Him** all that were diseased, and them that were possessed with devils. And all the city was gathered together at the door. And **He** healed many that were sick of divers diseases, and cast out many devils; and suffered not the devils to speak, because they knew **Him** howbeit they saith:

"Let us alone; what have we to do with **Thee, Thou Jesus of Nazareth?**" the unclean spirit said. In the eyes of

He heals Simon Peter's mother-in-law and reveals the hatred of the Pharisees!

the demoniac I could see **Him** not dressed in a coat without seam, woven from the top throughout, but a glorious fuchsia cloak armed with a golden staff with the graven image of **His** crucifixion upon the headpiece. What manner of sorcery? And the unclean spirit proclaimeth, "Art **Thou** come to destroy us? I know **Thee** who **Thou** art, the **Holy One of God**."

What kind of salutation is this from a demoniac? Refuseth I to believe this disbelief! Verily, this fellow doth not cast out devils, but by Beelzebub the prince of the devils!

And when it was day, **He** departed and went into a desert place: and the people sought **Him**, and came unto **Him**, and stayed **Him**, that **He** should not depart from them. And **He** said unto them, **"I must preach the kingdom of God to other cities also: for therefore am I sent."**

And **He** went about all Galilee, teaching in their synagogues, and preaching the gospel of the kingdom, and healing all manner of sickness and all manner of disease among the people. And **His** fame went throughout all Syria: and they brought unto **Him** all sick people, charlatans no doubt purchased by his purse, that were assumed to be inflected with divers diseases and torments; and those players acting upon the stage, which allege their possession by devils; and those which were lunatick, but sane— sinful, shameful charlatans, but sane — and those that had the palsy and a fraudulent limp and a fruitless crutch; and **He** healed them all, indubitably palming them shekels. This mountebank sold not counterfeit elixirs to the rural rubes. This quacksalver masqueraded as a holy one of **God** healing but with only a silver tongue.

And there followed **Him** great multitudes of people from Galilee, and from Decapolis, and from Jerusalem, and from Judaea, and from beyond Jordan.

And it came to pass, when **He** was in a certain city, behold a man full of leprosy, who seeing **Him** fell on his face, and besought **Him**, saying, "**Lord**, if **Thou** wilt, **Thou** canst make me clean." And **He** put forth **His** hand, and touched him, saying, **"I will: be thou clean."** And immediately the leprosy departed from him. And **He** charged him to tell no man: **"But go, and shew thyself to the priest, and offer for thy cleansing, according as Moses commanded:"**

And Moses Lawgiver thus commanded: "This shall be the law of the leper in the day of his cleansing: He shall be brought unto the priest: And the priest shall go forth out of the camp; and the priest shall look, and, behold, if the plague of leprosy be healed in the leper; then shall the priest command to take for him that is to be cleansed two birds alive and clean, and cedar wood, and scarlet, and hyssop: And the priest shall command that one of the birds be killed in an earthen vessel over running water: As for the living bird, he shall take it, and the cedar wood, and the scarlet, and the hyssop, and shall dip them and the living bird in the blood of the bird that was killed over the running water: And he shall sprinkle upon him that is to be cleansed from the leprosy seven times, and shall pronounce him clean, and shall let the living bird loose into the open field. And he that is to be cleansed shall wash his clothes, and shave off all his hair, and wash himself in water, that he may be clean: and after that he shall come into the camp, and shall tarry abroad out of his tent seven days. But it shall be on the seventh day, that he shall shave all his hair off his head and his beard and his eyebrows, even all his hair he shall shave off: and he shall wash his clothes, also he shall wash his flesh in water, and he shall be clean.

"And on the eighth day he shall take two he lambs

without blemish, and one ewe lamb of the first year without blemish, and three tenth deals of fine flour for a meat offering, mingled with oil, and one log of oil. And the priest that maketh him clean shall present the man that is to be made clean, and those things, before the LORD, at the door of the tabernacle of the congregation: And the priest shall take one he lamb, and offer him for a trespass offering, and the log of oil, and wave them for a wave offering before the LORD: and he shall slay the lamb in the place where he shall kill the sin offering and the burnt offering, in the holy place: for as the sin offering is the priest's, so is the trespass offering: it is most holy: And the priest shall take some of the blood of the trespass offering, and the priest shall put it upon the tip of the right ear of him that is to be cleansed, and upon the thumb of his right hand, and upon the great toe of his right foot: And the priest shall take some of the log of oil, and pour it into the palm of his own left hand: And the priest shall dip his right finger in the oil that is in his left hand, and shall sprinkle of the oil with his finger seven times before the LORD: And of the rest of the oil that is in his hand shall the priest put upon the tip of the right ear of him that is to be cleansed, and upon the thumb of his right hand, and upon the great toe of his right foot, upon the blood of the trespass offering: And the remnant of the oil that is in the priest's hand he shall pour upon the head of him that is to be cleansed: and the priest shall make an atonement for him before the LORD.

"And the priest shall offer the sin offering, and make an atonement for him that is to be cleansed from his uncleanness; and afterward he shall kill the burnt offering: And the priest shall offer the burnt offering and the meat offering upon the altar: and the priest shall make an atonement for him, and he shall be clean.

"And if he be poor, and cannot get so much; then he shall take one lamb for a trespass offering to be waved, to make an atonement for him, and one tenth deal of fine flour mingled with oil for a meat offering, and a log of oil; And two turtledoves, or two young pigeons, such as he is able to get; and the one shall be a sin offering, and the other a burnt offering. And he shall bring them on the eighth day for his cleansing unto the priest, unto the door of the tabernacle of the congregation, before the LORD. And the priest shall take the lamb of the trespass offering, and the log of oil, and the priest shall wave them for a wave offering before the LORD: And he shall kill the lamb of the trespass offering, and the priest shall take some of the blood of the trespass offering, and put it upon the tip of the right ear of him that is to be cleansed, and upon the thumb of his right hand, and upon the great toe of his right foot: And the priest shall pour of the oil into the palm of his own left hand: And the priest shall sprinkle with his right finger some of the oil that is in his left hand seven times before the LORD: And the priest shall put of the oil that is in his hand upon the tip of the right ear of him that is to be cleansed, and upon the thumb of his right hand, and upon the great toe of his right foot, upon the place of the blood of the trespass offering: And the rest of the oil that is in the priest's hand he shall put upon the head of him that is to be cleansed, to make an atonement for him before the LORD. And he shall offer the one of the turtledoves, or of the young pigeons, such as he can get; Even such as he is able to get, the one for a sin offering, and the other for a burnt offering, with the meat offering: and the priest shall make an atonement for him that is to be cleansed before the LORD. This is the law of him in whom is the plague of leprosy, whose hand is not able to get that which pertaineth to his cleansing."

But so much the more went there a fame abroad of **Him**: and great multitudes came together to hear, and to be healed by **Him** of their infirmities. And **He** withdrew **Himself** into the wilderness, and prayed.

And it came to pass on a certain day, as **He** was teaching, that there were Pharisees and doctors of the law sitting by, which were come out of every town of Galilee, and Judaea, and Jerusalem: and the power of the **LORD** was present to heal them. And, behold, men brought in a bed a man which was taken with a palsy, in truth a charlatan whom feigned lameness begging for alms in the shadow of the synagogue from the pious and the righteous, a sluggard whom doth not plow in season so at harvest time they look, but find nothing.

And the men sought means to bring him in, and to lay him before **Him**. And when they could not find by what way they might bring him in because of the multitude, they went upon the housetop, and let him down through the tiling with his couch into the midst before **Him**. And when **He** saw their faith, **He** said unto him, **"Man, thy sins are forgiven thee."**

And the elders and Pharisees and the Sadducees began to reason aloud so that all could hear the reasoning in their hearts and learneth a lesson in the Law, saying, "Who is this which speaketh blasphemies? Who can forgive sins, but **God** alone? Doth not Moses Lawgiver say, 'And Aaron's sons shall burn it on the altar upon the burnt sacrifice, which is upon the wood that is on the fire: it is an offering made by fire, of a sweet savour unto the **LORD**.' " And what is this sweet savour that is so pleasing unto the **LORD**? " 'He shall take away all the fat thereof, as the fat is taken away from off the sacrifice of peace offerings; and the priest shall burn it upon the altar for a sweet savour unto the **LORD**; and the priest shall make an atonement for him, and it shall be forgiven him.' Therefore only the sweet savour pleases the **LORD** to forgiveth sins!"

But when **He** heard their words and perceived their innermost thoughts, **He** answering said unto them, **"What reason ye in your hearts? Whether is easier, to say, 'Thy sins be forgiven thee'; or to say, 'Rise up and walk'? But that ye may know that the Son of man hath power upon earth to forgive sins"**, (**He** said unto the sick of the palsy,) **"I say unto thee, arise, and take up thy couch, and go into thine house."**

And immediately he rose up before them, and took up that whereon he lay, and departed to his own house, glorifying **God**. And they were all amazed, and they glorified **God**, and were filled with fear, saying, "We have seen strange things to-day!"

All this sorcery and charlatanry so that **He** might be the fulfillment which was spoken by Isaiah the prophet, saying, "Say to them that are of a fearful heart, 'Be strong, fear not: behold, your **God** will come with vengeance, even **God** with a recompence; **He** will come and save you.' Then the eyes of the blind shall be opened, and the ears of the deaf shall be unstopped. Then shall the lame man leap as an hart, and the tongue of the dumb sing: for in the wilderness shall waters break out, and streams in the desert."

Now when he had ended all **His** sayings in the audience of the people, **He** entered into Capernaum, the seat of **His** ministry. And a certain centurion's servant, who was dear unto him, was sick, and ready to die. And when he heard of **Him**, he sent unto **Him** the elders of the Jews, beseeching **Him** that **He** would come and heal his servant. And when they came to **Him**, they besought **Him** instantly, saying that he was worthy for whom **He** should do this: "For he loveth our nation, and he hath built us a synagogue."

Then **He** went with them. And when **He** was now not far from the house, the centurion sent friends to **Him**, saying unto **Him**, "Lord, trouble not **Thyself**: for I am not worthy that **Thou** shouldest enter under my roof: wherefore neither thought I myself worthy to come unto **Thee**: but say in a word, and my servant shall be healed. For I also am a man set under authority, having under me soldiers, and I say unto one, 'Go', and he goeth; and to another, 'Come', and he cometh; and to my servant, 'Do this', and he doeth it."

When **He** heard these things, **He** marvelled at him, and turned him about, and said unto the people that followed **Him**, **"I say unto you, I have not found so great faith, no, not in Israel!"** And they that were sent, returning to the house, found the servant whole that had been sick.

And it came to pass the day after, that **He** went into a city called Nain; and many of **His** disciples went with **Him**, and much people. Now when **He** came nigh to the gate of the city, behold, there was a dead man carried out, the only son of his mother, and she was a widow: and much people of the city was with her. When the **He** saw her, **He** had compassion on her, and said unto her, **"Weep not."** And **He** came and touched the bier: and they that bare him stood still. And **He** said, **"Young man, I say unto thee, Arise!"** And he that was dead sat up, and began to speak. And **He** delivered him to his mother.

He *heals the centurion's servant and reveals the honest faith of the Gentile!*

And there came a fear on all: and they glorified God, saying, that "A great prophet is risen up among us"; and "The **LORD** thy **God** will raise up unto thee a **Prophet** from the midst of thee, of thy brethren, like unto me; unto Him ye shall hearken"; and that "**God** hath visited **His** people." And this rumour of **Him** spread like a fire fanned by the scorching desert winds throughout all Judaea, and throughout all the region round about.

And after these things **He** went forth, and saw a publican, named Matthew, sitting at the receipt of custom: and he said unto him, **"Follow Me"**. And he left all, rose up, and followed **Him**.

And Matthew made him a great feast in his own house: and there was a great company of publicans and of others that sat down with them. But their scribes and Pharisees murmured against his disciples, saying, "Why do ye eat and drink with publicans and sinners?"

And **He** answering said unto them, **"They that are whole need not a physician; but they that are sick. I came not to call the righteous, but sinners to repentance."**

And the disciples of John and of the Pharisees used to fast and they said unto **Him**, "Why do the disciples of John fast often, and make prayers, and likewise the disciples of the Pharisees; but thine eat and drink?"

And **He** said unto them, **"Can ye make the children of the bridechamber fast, while the bridegroom is with them? But the days will come, when the bridegroom shall be taken away from them, and then shall they fast in those days."**

And **He** spake also a parable unto them: **"No man putteth a piece of a new garment upon an old; if otherwise, then both the new maketh a rent, and the piece that was taken out of the new agreeth not with the old. And** no man putteth new wine into old bottles; else the new wine will burst the bottles, and be spilled, and the bottles shall perish. But new wine must be put into new bottles; and both are preserved. No man also having drunk old wine straightway desireth new: for he saith, 'The old is better.' "

Chapter 5
"Blasphemy on the Mount"

EEING THE MULTITUDES, HE went up into a mountain: and when **He** was set, **His** disciples came unto **Him**: and **He** opened **His** heretical mouth, and taught them deceptions, saying:

"Blessed are the poor in spirit: for theirs is the kingdom of heaven. Blessed are they that mourn: for they shall be comforted. Blessed are the meek: for they shall inherit the earth. Blessed are they which do hunger and thirst after righteousness: for they shall be filled. Blessed are the merciful: for they shall obtain mercy. Blessed are the pure in heart: for they shall see God. Blessed are the peacemakers: for they shall be called the children of God. Blessed are they which are persecuted for righteousness' sake: for theirs is the kingdom of heaven. Blessed are ye, when men shall revile you, and persecute you, and

55

shall say all manner of evil against you falsely, for My sake. Rejoice, and be exceeding glad: for great is your reward in heaven: for so persecuted they the prophets which were before you.

"Ye are the salt of the earth: but if the salt have lost his savour, wherewith shall it be salted? it is thenceforth good for nothing, but to be cast out, and to be trodden under foot of men.

"Ye are the light of the world. A city that is set on an hill cannot be hid. Neither do men light a candle, and put it under a bushel, but on a candlestick; and it giveth light unto all that are in the house. Let your light so shine before men, that they may see your good works, and glorify your Father which is in heaven." Curiouser and curiouser! What manner of false prophet and misleading Messiah doth this Jesus of Nazareth of the Galilee be?

"Think not that I am come to destroy the law, or the prophets: I am not come to destroy, but to fulfil." Thinkest thou honourable Caiaphas that this should ease a wary mind, but lo! this deceitful Messiah is replete with false doctrines that fly and deny the LORD God of Israel that we alone speak for. He destroys the sabbatical law set down in stone by Moses Lawgiver on the mount of Sinai by His heretical healings on the eternal day of rest! And He mocks the prophets with His false fulfilments of the Messianic prophesies that are alone for the true Messiah to fulfil and not this false prophet whom stands in our very midst. We alone knowest when the Messiah shalt arise and we alone shalt deem said Israelite as the Messiah. We alone! And He continueth his heresy saying, "For verily I say unto you, 'Till heaven and earth pass, one jot or one tittle shall in no wise pass from the law, till all be fulfilled. Whosoever therefore shall break one of these least commandments, and shall teach men so, he shall be called the least in the kingdom of heaven: but whosoever shall do and teach them, the same shall be called great in the kingdom of heaven.' For I say unto you, 'That except your righteousness shall exceed the righteousness of the scribes and Pharisees, ye shall in no case enter into the kingdom of heaven.' " For I bear ye record that we have a zeal of God, but not according to knowledge. For we are ignorant of God's righteousness, and going about to establish our own righteousness, have not submitted ourselves unto the righteousness of God. He believeth He is the end of the law for righteousness to every one that believeth! And having abolished in His flesh the enmity, even the law of commandments contained in ordinances; for to make in himself of twain one new man, so making peace. And! He believeth that before He came, we were kept under the Law, shut up unto the faith which should afterwards be revealed. Wherefore the law was our schoolmaster to bring us unto Him, that we might be justified by faith. But after that faith is come, we should no longer be under a schoolmaster. Believeth this He and His sycophants do!

"Ye have heard that it was said of them of old time, 'Thou shalt not kill; and whosoever shall kill shall be in danger of the judgment': But I say unto you, that whosoever is angry with his brother without a cause shall be in danger of the judgment: and whosoever shall say to his brother, "Raca!" shall be in danger of the council: but whosoever shall say, "Thou fool!" shall be in danger of hell fire' Therefore if thou bring thy gift to the altar, and there rememberest that thy brother hath ought against thee; leave there thy gift before the altar, and go thy way; first be reconciled to thy brother, and then come and offer thy gift. Agree with thine adversary quickly, whiles thou art in the way with him; lest at any time the adversary deliver thee to the judge, and the judge deliver thee to the officer, and thou be cast into prison. Verily I say unto thee, 'Thou shalt by no means come out thence, till thou hast paid the uttermost farthing.'

"Ye have heard that it was said by them of old time, 'Thou shalt not commit adultery': But I say unto you, 'That whosoever looketh on a woman to lust after her hath committed adultery with her already in his heart.' " Didst not God bless Adam and Eve, and saith unto them, "Be fruitful, and multiply, and replenish the earth, and subdue it: and have dominion over the fish of the sea, and over the fowl of the air, and over every living thing that moveth upon the earth"? And! if we seest among our captives a beautiful woman, and hast a desire unto her, that thou wouldest have her to our wife, the LORD giveth us her! The LORD giveth us her! "If thy phallus offend thee, pluck it out, and cast it from thee: for it is profitable for thee that one of thy members should perish, and not that thy whole body should be cast into hell." Hikiah the high priest bringeth the wooden idol of Asherah and his phallus out of the house of the Lord, without Jerusalem, unto the brook Kidron, and burned it at the brook Kidron, and stamped it small to powder, and cast the powder thereof upon the graves of the children of the people. We faithful to the LORD God of Israel worship not the phallus as the heathen doeth! But! is not the members of our membership essential to be fruitful and multiply our nation?

"It hath been said, 'Whosoever shall put away his wife, let him give her a writing of divorcement': But I say unto you, that whosoever shall put away his wife, saving for the cause of fornication, causeth her to commit adultery: and whosoever shall marry her that is divorced committeth adultery."

Where it hath been said that the LORD our God forbids us to bear false witness against our neighbour, we, the elders and the chief priests and the scribes, will in good time bear honest and honourable witness against the false Messiah when it shall come to pass, that when He had finished many sayings, He departed from the Galilee, and came into the coasts of Judaea beyond Jordan. And great multitudes followed Him; and He healed them there. Our fellow Pharisees also came unto Him, challenging Him, and saying unto Him, "Is it lawful for a man to put away his wife for every cause?" And the Pharisees came to Him, and asked Him, "Is it lawful for a man to put away his wife?" disputing Him and His teachings. And He answered and said unto them, "What did Moses Lawgiver command you?" And our fellows said, "Moses suffered to write a bill of divorcement, and to put her away". And He answered and said unto them, "For the hardness of your heart he wrote you this precept. Have ye not read, that he which made them at the beginning made them male and female, and said, 'For this cause shall a man leave father and mother, and shall cleave to his wife: and they twain shall be one flesh?' Wherefore they are no more twain, but one flesh. What therefore God hath joined together, let not man put asunder." They say unto Him, "Why did Moses then command to give a writing of divorcement, and to put her away?" He saith unto them, "Moses because of the hardness of your hearts suffered you to put away your wives: but from the beginning it was not so. And I say unto you, whosoever shall put away his wife, except it be for fornication, and shall marry another, committeth adultery: and whoso marrieth her which is put away doth commit adultery." Even **His** disciples say unto **Him**, "If the case of the man be so with his wife, it is not good to marry."

And **He** continueth **His** sermon on the mount, "Again, ye have heard that it hath been said by them of old time, thou shalt not forswear thyself, but shalt perform unto the Lord thine oaths: but I say unto you, swear not at all; neither by heaven; for it is God's throne: nor by the earth; for it is his footstool: neither by Jerusalem; for it is the city of the great King. Neither shalt thou swear by thy head, because thou canst not make one hair white or black. But let your communication be, 'Yea, yea'; 'Nay, nay': for whatsoever is more than these cometh of evil.

"Ye have heard that it hath been said, 'An eye for an eye, and a tooth for a tooth': But I say unto you, that ye resist not evil: but whosoever shall smite thee on thy right cheek, turn to him the other also." Out of context are **His** teachings! This offender was the son of an Egyptian father, and an Israelitish mother. The notice of his parents shows the common ill effect of mixed marriages. A standing law for the stoning of blasphemers was made upon this occasion. Great stress is laid upon this law. It extends to the strangers among them, as well as to those born in the land. Strangers, as well as native Israelites, should be entitled to the benefit of the law, so as not to suffer wrong; and should be liable to the penalty of this law, in case they did wrong. If those who profane the name of **God** escape punishment from men, yet the **LORD** our **God** will not suffer them to escape his righteous judgments. What enmity against **God** must be in the heart of man, when blasphemies against **God** proceed out of his mouth. If he that despised Moses' law, died without mercy, of what punishment will they be worthy, who despise and abuse the **Word of God**! Let us watch against anger, do no evil, avoid all connexions with wicked people, and reverence that holy name which sinners blaspheme[1]. **"And if any man will sue thee at the law, and take away thy coat, let him have thy cloak also."** This is not **His** law to maketh judgments or be the judge whom maketh decrees upon the Law of Moses Lawgiver. The elders are the judges. The chief priests are the judges. The scribes are the judges. Not a carpenter from the Galilee! **"And whosoever shall compel thee to go a mile, go with him twain. Give to him that asketh thee, and from him that would borrow of thee turn not thou away.**

"Ye have heard that it hath been said, 'Thou shalt love thy neighbour, and hate thine enemy.' " Howbeit this is not the Law as given by Moses Lawgiver whom saith, "love your neighbor as yourself," with nary any hate of our enemies. Wherefore doth this **false Messiah** adulterate the **Word of God** and deceiveth the multitudes? **"But I say unto you, love your enemies, bless them that curse you, do good to them that hate you, and pray for them which despitefully use you, and persecute you; that ye may be the children of your Father which is in heaven: for He maketh His sun to rise on the evil and on the good, and sendeth rain on the just and on the unjust. For if ye love them which love you, what reward have ye? do not even the publicans the same? And if ye salute your brethren only, what do ye more than others? do not even the publicans so? Be ye therefore perfect, even as your Father which is in heaven is perfect."** Twisteth! And distorteth! the **Word of the LORD**. Deceiveth! **He** does the multitudes! **He** doth destroy the very law **He** saith **He** cometh not

---

1   Henry, Matthew, *Commentary on the Whole Bible*, abridged

to destroy nor the prophets!

"Take heed that ye do not your alms before men, to be seen of them: otherwise ye have no reward of your Father which is in heaven. Therefore when thou doest thine alms, do not sound a trumpet before thee, as the hypocrites do in the synagogues and in the streets, that they may have glory of men. Verily I say unto you, they have their reward. But when thou doest alms, let not thy left hand know what thy right hand doeth: that thine alms may be in secret: and thy Father which seeth in secret himself shall reward thee openly. And when thou prayest, thou shalt not be as the hypocrites are: for they love to pray standing in the synagogues and in the corners of the streets, that they may be seen of men." He dares to call the elders and the chief priests and the scribes hypocrites as did the Baptizer. We are not vipers in the bulrushes of the Jordan! We are the Pharisees and the Sadducees and the Sanhedrin of the nation of Israel! "Verily I say unto you, they have their reward. But thou, when thou prayest, enter into thy closet, and when thou hast shut thy door, pray to thy Father which is in secret; and thy Father which seeth in secret shall reward thee openly. But when ye pray, use not vain repetitions, as the heathen do: for they think that they shall be heard for their much speaking." He dares raise a closet over the impressive heights of the Temple?

"Be not ye therefore like unto them: for your Father knoweth what things ye have need of, before ye ask Him. After this manner therefore pray ye: Our Father which art in heaven, hallowed be Thy name. Thy kingdom come, Thy will be done in earth, as it is in heaven. Give us this day our daily bread. And forgive us our debts, as we forgive our debtors. And lead us not into temptation, but deliver us from evil: For thine is the kingdom, and the power, and the glory, for ever. Amen.

"For if ye forgive men their trespasses, your heavenly Father will also forgive you: But if ye forgive not men their trespasses, neither will your Father forgive your trespasses.

"Moreover when ye fast, be not, as the hypocrites, of a sad countenance: for they disfigure their faces, that they may appear unto men to fast. Verily I say unto you, they have their reward. But thou, when thou fastest, anoint thine head, and wash thy face; that thou appear not unto men to fast, but unto thy Father which is in secret: and thy Father, which seeth in secret, shall reward thee openly." And His disciples shouldst not eat corn upon the sabbath and He shouldst not defendeth them when they art undefendable.

"Lay not up for yourselves treasures upon earth, where moth and rust doth corrupt, and where thieves break through and steal: but lay up for yourselves treasures in heaven, where neither moth nor rust doth corrupt, and where thieves do not break through nor steal: for where your treasure is, there will your heart be also. The light of the body is the eye: if therefore thine eye be single, thy whole body shall be full of light. But if thine eye be evil, thy whole body shall be full of darkness. If therefore the light that is in thee be darkness, how great is that darkness! No man can serve two masters: for either he will hate the one, and love the other; or else he will hold to the one, and despise the other. Ye cannot serve God and mammon." He hath rendereth the tithes as commanded by the LORD as the work of Mammon. Behold, the LORD have given the children of Levi all the tenth in Israel for an inheritance, for their service which they serve, even the service of the tabernacle of the congregation! Didst not the LORD bless Abraham and saith, **"Blessed be Abram of the most high God, possessor of heaven and earth: and blessed be the most high God, which hath delivered thine enemies into thy hand"**? And did not Abraham giveth **Him** tithes of all.

"Judge not, that ye be not judged. For with what judgment ye judge, ye shall be judged: and with what measure ye mete, it shall be measured to you again. And why beholdest thou the mote that is in thy brother's eye, but considerest not the beam that is in thine own eye? Or how wilt thou say to thy brother, 'Let me pull out the mote out of thine eye'; and, behold, a beam is in thine own eye? Thou hypocrite, first cast out the beam out of thine own eye; and then shalt thou see clearly to cast out the mote out of thy brother's eye. Give not that which is holy unto the dogs, neither cast ye your pearls before swine, lest they trample them under their feet, and turn again and rend you.

"Beware of false prophets," saith the falsest of prophets, "which come to you in sheep's clothing, but inwardly they are ravening wolves. Ye shall know them by their fruits. Do men gather grapes of thorns, or figs of thistles? Even so every good tree bringeth forth good fruit; but a corrupt tree bringeth forth evil fruit. A good tree cannot bring forth evil fruit, neither can a corrupt tree bring forth good fruit. Every tree that bringeth not forth good fruit is hewn down, and cast into the fire. Wherefore by their fruits ye shall know them." He knoweth **Him** by **His** multitudes! The poor in spirit? They that mourn? The meek? They which do hunger and thirst after righteoiusness? The merciful? The pure of heart? The peacemakers? They which are persecuted for right-eousness sake? Bah! It is a humbug I tell thee!

"Not every one that saith unto Me, 'Lord, Lord', shall enter into the kingdom of heaven; but he that doeth the will of My Father which is in heaven. Many will say to Me in that day, 'Lord, Lord, have we not prophesied in Thy name? and in Thy name have cast out devils? and in Thy name done many wonderful works?' And then will I profess unto them, 'I never knew you: depart from Me, ye that work iniquity!'

"Therefore whosoever heareth these sayings of Mine, and doeth them, I will liken him unto a wise man, which built his house upon a rock: and the rain descended, and the floods came, and the winds blew, and beat upon that house; and it fell not: for it was founded upon a rock.

"And every one that heareth these sayings of Mine, and doeth them not, shall be likened unto a foolish man, which built his house upon the sand: and the rain descended, and the floods came, and the winds blew, and beat upon that house; and it fell: and great was the fall of it."

And it came to pass, when He had ended these sayings, the people were astonished at his doctrine: For He taught them as one having authority, and not as the scribes. When He was come down from the mountain, great multitudes followed Him. ✠

Chapter 6
"Sabbath Bloody Sabbath"

 E WENT ON THE SABBATH DAY through the corn; and **His** disciples were an hungred, and began to pluck the ears of corn and to eat. But when the Pharisees saw it, my brethren said unto **Him**, "Behold, **Thy** disciples do that which is not lawful to do upon the sabbath day."

And the elders and the chief priests and the scribes, who keepeth the word breathed by **God** into Moses Lawgiver, sat down respectfully to teacheth this rumoured Rabbi, saying the very words taught by the LORD, "Remember the sabbath day, to keep it holy. Six days shalt thou labour, and do all thy work: But the seventh day is the sabbath of the LORD thy God: in it thou shalt not do any work, thou, nor thy son, nor thy daughter, thy manservant, nor thy maidservant, nor thy cattle, nor thy stranger that is within thy gates: for in six days the LORD made heaven and

66

earth, the sea, and all that in them is, and rested the seventh day: wherefore the LORD blessed the sabbath day, and hallowed it."

While a selection of the Pharisees sought to con-descend with the very scripture, others taught a lesson from the very scripture, teaching, "And while the chil-dren of Israel were in the wilderness, they found a man that gathered sticks upon the sabbath day. And they that found him gathering sticks brought him unto Moses and Aaron, and unto all the congregation. And they put him in ward, because it was not declared what should be done to him.

"And the LORD said unto Moses, 'The man shall be surely put to death: all the congregation shall stone him with stones without the camp.' And all the congrega-tion brought him without the camp, and stoned him with stones, and he died; as the LORD commanded Moses."

Howbeit He said with stubbornness unto them and desirous of them not to stone His disciples which is their righteous right and privilege, "Have ye not read what Da-vid did, when he was an hungred, and they that were with him; how he entered into the house of God, and did eat the shewbread, which was not lawful for him to eat, neither for them which were with him, but only for the priests? Or have ye not read in the Law, how that on the sabbath days the priests in the temple profane the sab-bath, and are blameless? But I say unto you, that in this place is one greater than the temple. But if ye had known what this meaneth, I will have mercy, and not sacrifice, ye would not have condemned the guiltless. For the Son of man is LORD even of the sabbath day."

And when He was departed thence, He went into their synagogue: And, behold, there was a man which had his hand withered. And they asked **Him**, saying, "Is it lawful to heal on the sabbath days?" that they might accuse him.

And **He** said unto them, **"What man shall there be among you, that shall have one sheep, and if it fall into a pit on the sabbath day, will he not lay hold on it, and lift it out? How much then is a man better than a sheep? Wherefore it is lawful to do well on the sabbath days."** Then saith **He** to the man, **"Stretch forth thine hand."** And he stretched it forth; and it was restored whole, like as the other.

Then the Pharisees went out, and held a council against **Him**, how they might destroy **Him**.

But **He** withdrew himself with **His** disciples to the sea: and a great multitude from Galilee followed him, and from Judaea, and from Jerusalem, and from Idumaea, and from beyond Jordan; and they about Tyre and Sidon, a great multitude, when they had heard what great things **He** did, came unto **Him**. And **He** spake to his disciples, that a small ship should wait on **Him** because of the multitude, lest they should throng **Him**. For **He** had healed many; insomuch that they pressed upon **Him** for to touch **Him**, as many as had plagues. And unclean spirits, when they saw **Him**, fell down before **Him**, and cried, saying, **"Thou** art the **Son of God."** And **He** straitly charged them that they should not make **Him** known. That it might be fulfilled which was spoken by Isaiah the prophet, saying:

" **'Behold my servant, whom I uphold; mine elect, in whom my soul delighteth; I have put my spirit upon him: He shall bring forth judgment to the Gentiles. He shall not cry, nor lift up, nor cause His voice to be heard in the street. A bruised reed shall He not break, and the smoking flax shall He not quench: He shall bring forth** judgment unto truth. He shall not fail nor be discouraged, till He have set judgment in the earth: and the isles shall wait for His law.'

"Thus saith God the LORD, He that created the heavens, and stretched them out; He that spread forth the earth, and that which cometh out of it; He that giveth breath unto the people upon it, and spirit to them that walk therein: 'I the LORD have called thee in righteousness, and will hold thine hand, and will keep Thee, and give thee for a covenant of the people, for a light of the Gentiles; to open the blind eyes, to bring out the prisoners from the prison, and them that sit in darkness out of the prison house. I am the LORD: that is My name: and My glory will I not give to another, neither My praise to graven images. Behold, the former things are come to pass, and new things do I declare: before they spring forth I tell you of them.' "

And He goeth up into a mountain, and calleth unto Him whom He would: and they came unto Him. And He ordained twelve, that they should be with Him, and that He might send them forth to preach, And to have power to heal sicknesses, and to cast out devils: And Simon He surnamed Peter; and James the son of Zebedee, and John the brother of James; and He surnamed them Boanerges, which is, "The sons of thunder". And Andrew, and Philip, and Bartholomew, and Matthew, and Thomas, and James the son of Alphaeus, and Thaddaeus, and Simon the Canaanite, and Judas Iscariot, which also betrayed Him: and they went into an house.

And one of the Pharisees desired Him that He would eat with him. And h He e went into the Pharisee's house, and sat down to meat. And, behold, a woman in the city, which was a sinner, when she knew that He sat at meat

in the Pharisee's house, brought an alabaster box of ointment, and stood at **His** feet behind **Him** weeping, and began to wash **His** feet with tears, and did wipe them with the hairs of her head, and kissed **His** feet, and anointed them with the ointment.

Now when the Pharisee which had bidden **Him** saw it, he spake within himself, saying, "This **Man**, if **He** were a prophet, would have known who and what manner of woman this is that toucheth **Him**: for she is a sinner. And **He** answering said unto him, **"Simon, I have somewhat to say unto thee."** And he saith, **"Master**, say on."

"There was a certain creditor which had two debtors: the one owed five hundred pence, and the other fifty. And when they had nothing to pay, he frankly forgave them both. Tell Me therefore, which of them will love him most?" Simon answered and said, "I suppose that he, to whom he forgave most." And **He** said unto him, **"Thou hast rightly judged."**

And **He** turned to the woman, and said unto Simon, **"Seest thou this woman? I entered into thine house, thou gavest Me no water for My feet: but she hath washed My feet with tears, and wiped them with the hairs of her head. Thou gavest Me no kiss: but this woman since the time I came in hath not ceased to kiss My feet. My head with oil thou didst not anoint: but this woman hath anointed My feet with ointment. Wherefore I say unto thee, her sins, which are many, are forgiven; for she loved much: but to whom little is forgiven, the same loveth little."** And **He** said unto her, **"Thy sins are forgiven. And they that sat at meat with him began to say within themselves, Who is this that forgiveth sins also?"** And **He** said to the woman, **"Thy faith hath saved thee; go in peace."**

The woman with the alabaster jar provokes Him into chastising the Pharisee!

And **He** and **His** disciples went into an house. And the multitude cometh together again, so that they could not so much as eat bread. And when his friends heard of it, they went out to lay hold on him: for they said, "He is beside himself. "

Then was brought unto **Him** one possessed with a devil, blind, and dumb: and **He** laid His hands upon the head of the poor soul and **He** breathed out laboured and scalding breath scolding the demon and **He** healed him, insomuch that the blind and dumb both spake and saw. And all the people were amazed, and said, "Is not this the son of David?"

But when the Pharisees heard it, they said, "This fellow doth not cast out devils, but by Beelzebub the prince of the devils."

And **He** feigned to know their thoughts, and said unto them, "**O! generation of vipers, how can ye, being evil, speak good things? for out of the abundance of the heart the mouth speaketh. A good man out of the good treasure of the heart bringeth forth good things: and an evil man out of the evil treasure bringeth forth evil things. But I say unto you, That every idle word that men shall speak, they shall give account thereof in the day of judgment. For by thy words thou shalt be justified, and by thy words thou shalt be condemned!**

"**Am I in league with Beelzebub? The prince of devils?**" He said dancing and prancing, chanting and ranting like a madman! "**Fie! Every kingdom divided against itself is brought to desolation; and every city or house divided against itself shall not stand: and if Satan cast out Satan, he is divided against himself; how shall then his kingdom stand? And if I by Beelzebub cast out devils, by whom do your children cast them out? therefore they** shall be your judges. But if I cast out devils by the Spirit of God, then the kingdom of God is come unto you. Or else how can one enter into a strong man's house, and spoil his goods, except he first bind the strong man? and then he will spoil his house. He that is not with Me is against Me; and he that gathereth not with Me scattereth abroad."

Often have I ruminated as the days turned into weeks concerning this rebuke of our fellows. Surely the false Messiah is of the mind that: Satan is so subtle, that he will never voluntarily quit his possession. If this false Messiah be the True Messiah therefore He seeketh war upon the devil's kingdom, and hath a direct tendency to break his power, and crush his interest in the souls of men; and it is as plain that the casting of him out of the bodies of people confirmed that doctrine, and gave it the setting on; and therefore it cannot be imagined that he should come into such a design; every one knows that Satan is no fool, nor will act so directly against his own interest[1].

Nay! Faith! Consider if Satan, subtle as he is, would ever voluntarily quit his possession. Yay! Have faith that Satan can without question cast out Satan without dividing himself and his kingdom can surely stand. The lesser devil will verily relinquish his minor and irritating possession of the unfortunate man to further the machinations of the false Messiah. By installing the false Messiah as the King of the land of Israel, Satan himself gains control of the Holy City, the Temple, and the Holy of Holies itself. The needs of the kingdom surely outweigh the needs of the commoner. Verily, the false Messiah seeks to feign the threat posed to our great nation through His rise by saying the city-state of Satan cannot stand if divided. Therefore, Yay! Have faith

---

1 Matthew Henry Commentary on Matthew 12:26

that Satan can without question cast out Satan!

And He continueth, "Wherefore I say unto you, all manner of sin and blasphemy shall be forgiven unto men: but the blasphemy against the Holy Ghost shall not be forgiven unto men. And whosoever speaketh a word against the Son of man, it shall be forgiven him: but whosoever speaketh against the Holy Ghost, it shall not be forgiven him, neither in this world, neither in the world to come.

"Either make the tree good, and his fruit good; or else make the tree corrupt, and his fruit corrupt: for the tree is known by his fruit."

Then certain of the scribes and of the Pharisees answered, saying, "Master, we would see a sign from Thee." But He answered and said unto them, "An evil and adulterous generation seeketh after a sign; and there shall no sign be given to it, but the sign of the prophet Jonas: For as Jonas was three days and three nights in the whale's belly; so shall the Son of man be three days and three nights in the heart of the earth. The men of Nineveh shall rise in judgment with this generation, and shall condemn it: because they repented at the preaching of Jonas; and, behold, a greater than Jonas is here. The queen of the south shall rise up in the judgment with this generation, and shall condemn it: for she came from the uttermost parts of the earth to hear the wisdom of Solomon; and, behold, a greater than Solomon is here.

"When the unclean spirit is gone out of a man, he walketh through dry places, seeking rest, and findeth none. Then he saith, 'I will return into my house from whence I came out'; and when he is come, he findeth it empty, swept, and garnished. Then goeth he, and taketh with himself seven other spirits more wicked than himself, and they enter in and dwell there: and the last state of that man is worse than the first. Even so shall it be also unto this wicked generation."

While he yet talked to the people, behold, his mother and his brethren stood without, desiring to speak with him. Then one said unto him, "Behold, Thy mother and Thy brethren stand without, desiring to speak with Thee." But he answered and said unto him that told him, "Who is My mother? and who are My brethren?" And He stretched forth His hand toward His disciples, and said, "Behold My mother and My brethren! For whosoever shall do the will of My Father which is in heaven, the same is My brother, and sister, and mother." And His mother and His brethren returned unto the city of their birth their hearts heavy and full of sadness for her Son and their Brother hath rejected them with spite, with wrath, with madness.

Then came together unto Him the Pharisees, and certain of the scribes, which came from Jerusalem. And when they saw some of His disciples eat bread with defiled, that is to say, with unwashen hands, they found fault. For the Pharisees, and all the Jews, except they wash their hands oft, eat not, holding the tradition of the elders. And when they come from the market, except they wash, they eat not. And many other things there be, which they have received to hold, as the washing of cups, and pots, brasen vessels, and of tables.

Then the Pharisees and scribes asked him, "Why walk not Thy disciples according to the tradition of the elders, but eat bread with unwashen hands?" **He** answered and said unto them, "**Well hath Isaiah prophesied of you hypocrites, as it is written, 'This people honoureth me with their lips, but their heart is far from me. Howbeit in vain do they worship Me, teaching for doctrines the commandments of men.' For laying aside the commandment of God, ye hold the tradition of men, as the washing of pots and cups: and many other such like things ye do."**

And **He** said unto them, "**Full well ye reject the commandment of God, that ye may keep your own tradition. For Moses Lawgiver said, 'Honour thy father and thy mother'; and, 'Whoso curseth father or mother, let him die the death': But ye say, 'If a man shall say to his father or mother, "It is Corban" ', that is to say, a gift, by whatsoever thou mightest be profited by me; he shall be free. And ye suffer him no more to do ought for his father or his mother; making the word of God of none effect through your tradition, which ye have delivered: and many such like things do ye."**

And when **He** had called all the people unto **Him**, **He** said unto them, "**Hearken unto Me every one of you, and understand: there is nothing from without a man, that entering into him can defile him: but the things which come out of him, those are they that defile the man. If any man have ears to hear, let him hear."**

And when **He** was entered into the house from the people, then came **His** disciples, and said unto **Him**, "Knowest thou that the Pharisees were offended, after they heard this saying?" But **He** answered and said, "**Every plant, which My heavenly Father hath not planted, shall be rooted up. Let them alone: they be blind leaders of the blind. And if the blind lead the blind, both shall fall into the ditch."**

Then answered Peter and said unto **Him**, "Declare unto us this parable." And **Him** said, **"Are ye also yet without understanding? Do ye not perceive, that whatsoever thing from without entereth into the man, it cannot defile him; because it entereth not into his heart, but into the belly, and goeth out into the draught, purging all meats?"** And **He** said, **"That which cometh out of the man, that defileth the man. For from within, out of the heart of men, proceed evil thoughts, adulteries, fornications, murders, thefts, covetousness, wickedness, deceit, lasciviousness, an evil eye, blasphemy, pride, foolishness: all these evil things come from within, and defile the man."**

After this there was a feast of the Jews; and **He** went up to Jerusalem. Now there is at Jerusalem by the sheep market a pool, which is called in the Hebrew tongue Bethesda, having five porches. In these lay a great multitude of impotent folk, of blind, halt, withered, waiting for the moving of the water. For an angel went down at a certain season into the pool, and troubled the water: whosoever then first after the troubling of the water stepped in was made whole of whatsoever disease he had. And a certain man was there, which had an infirmity thirty and eight years. When **He** saw him lie, and knew that he had been now a long time in that case, **He** saith unto him, **"Wilt thou be made whole?"**

The impotent man answered **Him**, **"Sir**, I have no man, when the water is troubled, to put me into the pool: but while I am coming, another steppeth down before me." And **He** saith unto him, **"Rise, take up thy bed, and** walk." And immediately the man was made whole, and took up his bed, and walked: and on the same day was the sabbath. Our fellows therefore said unto him that was cured, "It is the sabbath day: it is not lawful for thee to carry thy bed."

He answered them, "He that made me whole, the same said unto me, 'Take up thy bed, and walk.'" Then asked they him, "What Man is that which said unto thee, 'Take up thy bed, and walk?' " And he that was healed wist not who it was: for He had conveyed Himself away, a multitude being in that place. Afterward He findeth him in the temple, and said unto him, "Behold, thou art made whole: sin no more, lest a worse thing come unto thee." The man departed, and told the Jews that it was Him, which had made him whole.

And therefore did our fellows persecute Jesus of Nazareth of the Galilee, and sought to slay Him, because He had done these things on the sabbath day. Again and again on the sabbath day! But Jesus answered them, "My Father worketh hitherto, and I work." Therefore our fellows sought the more to kill Him, because He not only had broken the sabbath, but said also that God was His Father, making himself equal with God.

Then answered Him and said unto them, "Verily, verily, I say unto you, the Son can do nothing of Himself, but what He seeth the Father do: for what things soever He doeth, these also doeth the Son likewise. For the Father loveth the Son, and sheweth Him all things that Himself doeth: and He will shew Him greater works than these, that ye may marvel. For as the Father raiseth up the dead, and quickeneth them; even so the Son quickeneth whom He will. For the Father judgeth no man, but hath committed all judgment unto the Son: that all men should honour the Son, even as they honour the Father. He that honoureth not the Son honoureth not the Father which hath sent him.

"Verily, verily, I say unto you, he that heareth My word, and believeth on Him that sent Me, hath everlasting life, and shall not come into condemnation; but is passed from death unto life. Verily, verily, I say unto you, the hour is coming, and now is, when the dead shall hear the voice of the Son of God: and they that hear shall live. For as the Father hath life in Himself; so hath He given to the Son to have life in Himself; and hath given Him authority to execute judgment also, because He is the Son of man. Marvel not at this: for the hour is coming, in the which all that are in the graves shall hear His voice, and shall come forth; they that have done good, unto the resurrection of life; and they that have done evil, unto the resurrection of damnation. I can of Mine own self do nothing: as I hear, I judge: and My judgment is just; because I seek not Mine own will, but the will of the Father which hath sent Me.

"If I bear witness of Myself, My witness is not true. There is another that beareth witness of Me; and I know that the witness which he witnesseth of Me is true. Ye sent unto John, and he bare witness unto the truth. But I receive not testimony from man: but these things I say, that ye might be saved. He was a burning and a shining light: and ye were willing for a season to rejoice in his light. But I have greater witness than that of John: for the works which the Father hath given Me to finish, the same works that I do, bear witness of Me, that the Father hath sent Me. And the Father Himself, which hath sent Me, hath borne witness of Me. Ye have neither heard His voice at any time, nor seen His shape. And ye have not His word abiding in you: for whom He hath sent, Him ye believe not. Search the scriptures; for in them ye think ye have eternal life: and they are they which testify of Me. And ye will not come to Me, that ye might have life.

"I receive not honour from men. But I know you, that ye have not the love of God in you. I am come in My Father's name, and ye receive Me not: if another shall come in His own name, him ye will receive. How can ye believe, which receive honour one of another, and seek not the honour that cometh from God only? Do not think that I will accuse you to the Father: there is one that accuseth you, even Moses, in whom ye trust. For had ye believed Moses, ye would have believed Me; for he wrote of Me. But if ye believe not his writings, how shall ye believe My words?" ✝

Interlewd
"The Song of Salome"

**HE DISCIPLES OF JOHN CAME** upon **Him** whilst **He** was on **His** ministry in the Galilee. They told **Him** the woeful and lamentable tragedy that befell **His** cousin. Herod Antipas, the tetrarch, had laid hold on John, and bound him, and put him in prison for Herodias' sake, his brother Philip's wife. For John said unto him in his own court, with his wife and her daughter in attendance, "It is not lawful for thee to have her!" And the multitudes murmured amongst themselves at the brashness of the Baptizer, whom brazenly saith, "For knoweth I do the knowledge of the Law as bequeathed unto us by Moses Lawgiver. 'Thou shalt not uncover the nakedness of thy brother's wife: it is thy brother's nakedness and if a man shall take his brother's wife, it is an unclean thing: he hath uncovered his brother's nakedness; they shall be childless.' " And there were rum-

81

blings between the merchants and the exchangers of money because they knew Herodias, was once married to Philip, the son of Herod the Great, who was born of Mariamne, the daughter of Simon the high priest, who had a daughter, Salome; after whose birth Herodias took upon her to confound the laws of our country, and divorced herself from her husband while he was alive, and was married to Herod Antipas, her husband's brother by the father's side, he was tetrarch of Galilee[1]. And the guards were heightened in their readiness, due to the unashamed repudiations of the Baptizer against their tetrarch, "Ye wantonly and lasciviously disregard and dispute the Law with your displays and your adulterous marriage! For they that forsake the law praise the wicked: but such as keep the law contend with them. I have not troubled Israel; but thou, and thy father's house, in that ye have forsaken the commandments of the LORD, and thou hast followed Baalim."

Those assembled in the court who heard the accusations of the Baptizer against Herod Antipas and Herodias knew John was a good man, and commanded the Jews to exercise virtue, both as to righteousness towards one another, and piety towards God, and so to come to baptism; for that the washing with water would be acceptable to Him, if they made use of it, not in order to the putting away or the remission of some sins only, but for the purification of the body; supposing still that the soul was thoroughly purified beforehand by righteousness. Now when many others came in crowds about him, for they were very greatly moved or pleased by hearing his words, Herod, who feared lest the great influence John had over the people might put it into his power and inclination to raise a rebellion, (for they seemed ready to do any thing he should advise.)[2] And

---

1　Josephus, *Antiquities of the Jews*, book 18, chapter 5, paragraph 4
2　Ibid, book 18, chapter 5, paragraph 2

Herod Antipas would have put him to death, both
for inciting rebellion and for insulting his marriage,
howbeit, he feared the multitude, because they counted the Baptizer as a prophet.

But when Herod's birthday was kept, the daughter
of Herodias, sang a song of Solomon and danced a dance
of Salome, singing:

> Let him kiss me with the kisses of his mouth:
> For thy love is better than wine.
> Because of the savour of thy good ointments
> Thy name is as ointment poured forth,
> Therefore do the virgins love thee. Draw me!

Thus the song began and therefore the song continued with Salome dancing with beguile and shimmying with
seduction, writhing with allure, her heavy breasts heaving,
her serpentine hips coiling. Her dance delighted the court
and she titillated in a twisting tango with a beauteous young
man, whom possessed an alluring tenorous voice. As he ap-
proacheth the finale of the song of Solomon, he sang to the
seduced assembly:

> How fair and how pleasant art thou,
> O! love, for delights!
> This thy stature is like to a palm tree,
> And thy breasts to clusters of grapes.
> I will go up to the palm tree,
> I will take hold of the boughs thereof:
> Now also thy breasts shall be as clusters of the vine,
> And the smell of thy nose like apples;
> And the roof of thy mouth like the best wine.

And! Salome sang the final notes of Solomon's song that goeth done sweetly, causing the lips of those that are asleep to speak:

> *I am my beloved's,*
> *And his desire is toward me.*
> *Come, my beloved, let us go forth into the field;*
> *Let us lodge in the villages.*
> *Let us get up early to the vineyards;*
> *Let us see if the vine flourish,*
> *Whether the tender grape appear,*
> *And the pomegranates bud forth:*
> *There will I give thee my loves.*
> *The mandrakes give a smell,*
> *And at our gates are all manner*
> *Of pleasant fruits, new and old,*
> *Which I have laid up for thee, O! my beloved.*

And Salome pleased Herod. Whereupon he promised with an oath before the **LORD** his **God** to give her whatsoever she would ask. And she knoweth that if a man vow a vow unto the **LORD**, or swear an oath to bind his soul with a bond; he shall not break his word, he shall do according to all that proceedeth out of his mouth. Due to this sworn oath and being before instructed of her mother, said, "Give me here John the Baptist's head in a charger."

And the king was sorry: nevertheless for the oath's sake, and them which sat with him at meat, he commanded it to be given her. And he sent for John from to be brought from the putrid prison of the depths of the dungeons and into the prison of pure opulence that was Herod's court. The follow prisoners in the court of Herod, dressed in the silks and

---

Selome the seductress seduces her mother's husband into killing the Baptizer!

finery of lords and ladies and not the Godly raiment of camel's hair and a leathern girdle, were obliged to be witnesses the king in the keeping of his sworn oath.

And just as Herod kept his oath, the soldiers fulfilled their own when a solider bent John over to be beheaded over an ornate and carved bench. John prayed: "Give the king **Thy** judgments, O! **God**, and **Thy** righteousness unto the king's son. **He** shall judge **Thy** people with righteousness, and **Thy** poor with judgment. The mountains shall bring peace to the people, and the little hills, by righteousness. **He** shall judge the poor of the people, **He** shall save the children of the needy, and shall break in pieces the oppressor. They shall fear **Thee** as long as the sun and moon endure, throughout all generations. **He** shall come down like rain upon the mown grass: as showers that water the earth. In **His** days shall the righteous flourish; and abundance of peace so long as the moon endureth. **He** shall have dominion also from sea to sea, and from the river unto the ends of the earth. They that dwell in the wilderness shall bow before **Him**; and **His** enemies shall lick the dust. The kings of Tarshish and of the isles shall bring presents: the kings of Sheba and Seba shall offer gifts. Yea, all kings shall fall down before **Him**: all nations shall serve **Him**. For **He** shall deliver the needy when **He** crieth; the poor also, and **Him** that hath no helper. **He** shall spare the poor and needy, and shall save the souls of the needy. **He** shall redeem their soul from deceit and violence: and precious shall their blood be in **His** sight. And **He** shall live, and to **Him** shall be given of the gold of Sheba: prayer also shall be made for **Him** continually; and daily shall **He** be praised. There shall be an handful of corn in the earth upon the top of the mountains; the fruit thereof shall shake like Lebanon: and they of the city shall flourish like grass of the earth. **His** name shall endure for ever: **His** name shall be continued as long as the sun: and men shall be blessed in **Him**: all nations shall call **Him** blessed. Blessed be the **Lord God, the God of Israel**, who only doeth wondrous things. And blessed be **His** glorious name for ever: and let the whole earth be filled with **His** glory; Amen, and Amen."

The solider wielding the sharpened sword, arched rearward, and swung cleanly with a single swift blow and the head of John the Baptist was cleaved from his shoulders. The follow prisoners in the court of opulence gasped in their horror as the head rasped its last blood-gorged breath. And the head placed in a charger, and given to the damsel whom danced for and had entranced Herod: and she brought it to her mother, the wicked whorish Herodias. And the disciples of the Baptist came into the court, and took up the body, and buried it, and went far and wide into the Galilee and told **Him His** cousin was dead. ✝

Chapter 7
"Rejected After Feeding the 5,000 Counterfeitedly"

HEN HE LEARNED JOHN'S DIS-ciples hath came, and took up the body, and buried it, **He** said unto **His** disciples, **"Come ye yourselves apart into a desert place, and rest a while"**: for there were many coming and going, and they had no leisure so much as to eat, and they departed into a desert place by ship privately.

And the people saw them departing, and many knew **Him**, and ran afoot thither out of all cities, and outwent them, and came together unto **Him**. And **He**, when **He** came out, saw much people, and was moved with compassion toward them, because they were as sheep not having a shepherd: and **He** began to teach them many things. And when the day was now far spent, **His** disciples came unto **He**, and said, "This is a desert place, and now the time is far passed: send them away, that they may go into the country round about, and into the villages, and buy themselves bread: for they have nothing to eat." He answered and said unto them, **"Give ye them to eat."** And they say unto **Him**, "Shall we go and buy two hundred pennyworth of bread, and give them to eat?" **He** saith unto them, **"How many loaves have ye? go and see."**

An aged man, his raiment of camel's hair, and a leathern girdle about his loins, and his meat was locusts and wild honey, approached **Him** holding a stone hewn in twain and saith unto **Him**, "By what miracle this be! What other way I see not; for we here live on tough roots and stubs, to thirst inured more than the camel, and to drink go far– men to much misery and hardship born. But, if thou be the **Son of God**, command that out of these hard stones be made **Thee** bread; so shalt **Thou** save **Thyself**, and us relieve with food, whereof we wretched seldom taste." Howbeit, **He** ignored the aged man as if afeared of a unclean desert spirit full of malevolence.

One of **His** disciples, Andrew, Simon Peter's brother, saith unto **Him**, "There is a lad here, which hath five barley loaves, and two small fishes: but what are they among so many?" And **He** said, **"Make the men sit down"** by companies upon the green grass. And they sat down in ranks, by hundreds, and by fifties. And when **He** had taken the five loaves and the two fishes, **He** looked up to heaven, and blessed, and brake the loaves, and gave them to **His** disciples to set before them; and the two fishes divided **He** among them all. And they did all eat, and when they were filled, **He** said unto his disciples, **"Gather up the fragments that remain, that nothing be lost."** And they took up twelve baskets full of the fragments, and of the fishes. And they that did eat of the loaves were about five thousand men.

"But!" saith the aged man, "How therefore can Thy disciples gather the fragments of the five barley loaves, which remained over and fill twelve baskets? Is it not written man lives not by bread only, but each word proceeding from the mouth of God, who fed our fathers here with manna?" Bewildered, He gazed upon the aged man as if He hath a devil, and is mad, His eyes wild with the blindness of fear and lunacy. Who was this aged man to maketh Him so afeared, when He mocks our threatenings of death by stones with such derision and scorn?

Those multitudes, who were deceived by His charlatanry and conjury to believeth they were satiated by a mere five loaves and two small fishes, when they had seen the purported miracle that He did said, "This is of a truth that prophet that should come into the world." When He therefore perceived that they would come and take him by force, to make Him a king, He departed again into a mountain Himself alone.

The day following, when the people which stood on the other side of the sea saw that there was none other boat there, save that one whereinto His disciples were entered, and that He went not with His disciples into the boat, but that His disciples were gone away alone; (howbeit there came other boats from Tiberias nigh unto the place where they did eat bread, after that the Lord had given thanks:) When the people therefore saw that He was not there, neither His disciples, they also took shipping, and came to Capernaum, seeking for He. And when they had found Him

He confirms the Pharisees fears and uses the magicks of Beelzebub to feed the 5,000!

on the other side of the sea, the multitudes said unto Him, "Rabbi, when camest thou hither?"

He answered them and said, "Verily, verily, I say unto you, ye seek Me, not because ye saw the miracles, but because ye did eat of the loaves, and were filled. Labour not for the meat which perisheth, but for that meat which endureth unto everlasting life, which the Son of man shall give unto you: for him hath God the Father sealed."

Then said the curious aged man unto Him, "What shall we do, that we might ourselves work the works of God? How might Thee giveth us power against unclean spirits, to cast them out, and to heal all manner of sickness and all manner of disease, as Thou hast Thy disciples? That we might feed with a mere five loaves and two small fishes the multitudes whom were filled, and with twelve baskets in surplus? That we might open the eyes of the blind and unstop the ears of the deaf and maketh the lame man leap as a hart, and the tongue of the dumb sing. as it is written? That we might rebuke the devil and the spirit shalt cry and rent the unfortunate sore, and he shalt depart out of the unclean? That we might we taketh the dead by the hand, and saith unto them, '*Talitha cumi*', which is being interpreted, 'Damsel, I say unto the, arise,' and the dead shalt arise and walk with a great astonishment?" He answered not the aged man but spake unto the whole of the multitudes and said, "This is the work of God, that ye believe on Him whom He hath sent."

And the aged man said, "If we maketh Thee our LORD, which is our refuge, and we may setteth on a pinnacle of the temple, and cast ourselves down, wilt Thou give Thy angels charge over us, to keep us in all our ways. They shall bear us up in their hands, lest we dash our foot against a stone, for it is so written." His eyes were raving with madness beholding the aged man and He said unto the curious aged man, "Because I hath set My love upon Him, therefore will He deliver Me: He will set Me on high, because I hath known His name. I shall call upon Him, and He will answer Me: He will be with Me in trouble; He will deliver Me, and honour Me. With long life will He satisfy Me, and shew Me His salvation."

The aged man said therefore unto Him, "What sign shewest Thou then, that we may see, and believe Thee? what dost Thou work? Our fathers did eat manna in the desert; as it is written, 'He gave them bread from heaven to eat.' " Then He said unto the lot, "Verily, verily, I say unto you, Moses Lawgiver gave you not that bread from heaven; but My Father giveth you the true bread from heaven. For the bread of God is He which cometh down from heaven, and giveth life unto the world."

Then said the aged man unto Him, "Lord, evermore give us this bread." And He said unto the assembled, "I am the bread of life: he that cometh to Me shall never hunger; and he that believeth on Me shall never thirst. But I said unto you, that ye also have seen Me, and believe not. All that the Father giveth Me shall come to Me; and him that cometh to Me I will in no wise cast out. For I came down from heaven, not to do Mine own will, but the will of him that sent Me. And this is the Father's will which hath sent Me, that of all which He hath given Me I should lose nothing, but should raise it up again at the last day. And this is the will of Him that sent Me, that every one which seeth the Son, and believeth on Him, may have everlasting life: and I will raise him up at the last day."

The Jews then murmured at **Him**, because **He** said, "**I am the bread which came down from heaven.**" And the whole of the multitudes amongst themselves said, "Is not this **Jesus**, the son of Joseph, whose father and mother we know? how is it then that **He** saith, 'I came down from heaven?' "

He therefore answered and said unto them, "**Murmur not among yourselves. No man can come to Me, except the Father which hath sent Me draw him: and I will raise him up at the last day. It is written in the prophets, and they shall be all taught of God. Every man therefore that hath heard, and hath learned of the Father, cometh unto Me. Not that any man hath seen the Father, save he which is of God, he hath seen the Father. Verily, verily, I say unto you, he that believeth on Me hath everlasting life. I am that bread of life. Your fathers did eat manna in the wilderness, and are dead. This is the bread which cometh down from heaven, that a man may eat thereof, and not die. I am the living bread which came down from heaven: if any man eat of this bread, he shall live for ever: and the bread that I will give is My flesh, which I will give for the life of the world.**"

The Jews therefore strove among themselves, saying, "How can this man give us **His** flesh to eat?" Then **He** said unto them, "**Verily, verily, I say unto you, except ye eat the flesh of the Son of man, and drink His blood, ye have no life in you. Whoso eateth My flesh, and drinketh My blood, hath eternal life; and I will raise him up at the last day. For My flesh is meat indeed, and My blood is drink indeed. He that eateth My flesh, and drinketh My blood, dwelleth in Me, and I in him. As the living Father hath sent Me, and I live by the Father: so he that eateth Me, even he shall live by Me. This is that bread which came** down from heaven: not as your fathers did eat manna, and are dead: he that eateth of this bread shall live for ever."

What raving is this teaching? Only if we as a nation hearken not unto the LORD God of Israel, and walk contrary unto Him art we condemned to eat the flesh of our sons, and the flesh of our daughters shall we eat. In our oppression under the choke of Rome, shall our women eat their fruit, and children of a span long? No heathen god, not even the condemnable Molech, whom desireth to consume the seed of our nation in fire, desireth us eat of their flesh. This is heresy! This is blasphemy! This is lunacy!

Many therefore of His disciples, when they had heard this, said, "This is an hard saying; who can hear it?" Huzzah! Well said! There is wisdom yet found in this asylum! When He knew in Himself that His disciples murmured at it, He said unto them, "Doth this offend you? What and if ye shall see the Son of man ascend up where He was before? It is the spirit that quickeneth; the flesh profiteth nothing: the words that I speak unto you, they are spirit, and they are life. But there are some of you that believe not." For He knew from the beginning who they were that believed not, and who should betray Him. And He said, "Therefore said I unto you, that no man can come unto Me, except it were given unto him of My Father."

From that time many of His disciples went back, and walked no more with Him, but tarry must I to report unto the Sanhedrin His heresies. Howbeit how many of the five thousand, those to whom His charlatanry and conjury hath deceived now walk no more with Him? Five thousand! Five thousand who knoweth the knowledge that thus saith the LORD of hosts, "If there arise among you a prophet, or a dreamer of dreams, and giveth thee a sign or a wonder, and the sign or the wonder come to pass, whereof He spake unto thee, saying, 'I am the way, the truth, and the life: no man cometh unto the Father, but by Me. If ye had known Me, ye should have known My Father also: and from henceforth ye know Him, and have seen Him'; thou shalt not hearken unto the words of that prophet, or that dreamer of dreams: for the LORD your God proveth you, to know whether ye love the LORD your God with all your heart and with all your soul. Ye shall walk after the LORD your God, and fear Him, and keep His commandments, and obey His voice, and ye shall serve Him, and cleave unto Him. And that prophet, or that dreamer of dreams, shall be put to death; because He hath spoken to turn you away from the LORD your God, which brought you out of the land of Egypt, and redeemed you out of the house of bondage, to thrust thee out of the way which the LORD thy God commanded thee to walk in. So shalt thou put the evil away from the midst of thee." Only four score and three disciples remain! The twelve closest to **Him**, some seventy more, and myself are all that choose (or must acquiesce) to walk with a madman.

Then said **He** unto the twelve, **"Will ye also go away?"** Then Simon Peter answered **Him**, **"Lord**, to whom shall we go? **Thou** hast the words of eternal life. And we believe and are sure that **Thou** art that **Christ**, the **Son** of the living **God**." He answered them, **"Have not I chosen you twelve, and one of you is a devil?"** He seemed to speak of Judas Iscariot the son of Simon: howbeit **He** could knoweth not that I hath been in conspiracy with one of the twelve that he should, when the hour had come, betray **Him** unto thee, honourable Caiaphas.

Chapter 8
"On the Third Day, They Shalt Rob His Grave"

HEY DEPARTED THENCE, AND passed through Galilee; and **He** would not that any man should know it (except the twelve and the seventy and one whom feigns discipleship). And while they abode in Galilee, **He** taught **His** disciples, and said unto them, **"Behold, we go up to Jerusalem; and the Son of man shall be betrayed by one of you unto the chief priests and unto the scribes, and they shall condemn Him to death, and shall deliver Him to the Pontius Pilate to mock Him, and to scourge Him, and to crucify Him; they shalt make His grave with the wicked, and with the rich in His death and He shalt descend into and harrow Hell; and the third day He shall rise again!"** And they were exceeding sorry. But they understood not this saying, and it was hid from them, that they perceived it not: and they feared to ask **Him** of that saying.

His disciples knoweth not the knowledge of the most sacred of scriptures for thus saith the **LORD**, "But the prophet, which shall presume to speak a word in My name, which I have not commanded him to speak, or that shall speak in the name of other gods, even that prophet shall die. And if thou say in thine heart, 'How shall we know the word which the LORD hath not spoken?' When a prophet speaketh in the name of the LORD, if the thing follow not, nor come to pass, that is the thing which the Lord hath not spoken, but the prophet hath spoken it presumptuously: thou shalt not be afraid of him."

He possesseth the wisdom to presume his **false Messiahship** shalt incur the scrutiny, persecution, and execution due to the wrath of Rome and its governor Pontius Pilate, whose vindictiveness and furious temper is naturally inflexible, a blend of self-will and relentlessness and his corruption, and his acts of insolence, and his rapine, and his habit of insulting people, and his cruelty, and his continual murders of people untried and uncondemned, and his never ending, and gratuitous, and most grievous inhumanity[1].

Howbeit the latter prophecy that **He** shalt be resurrected of the dead is a humbug, for while many of them that sleep in the dust of the earth shall awake, some to everlasting life, and some to shame and everlasting contempt as shall befall this **false Messiah**. On the third day **He** shall be raised again? On the third day **He** shall be raised again! Fie! A pox upon **Him**!

Where-oh-where hath we heard this malarkey elsewhere? Hath **He** not saith in the Temple of our **LORD**, **"Destroy this temple, and in three days I will raise it up."** Fie! upon this revolutionary to believe **He** could raze the

---

1 Philo, *On The Embassy of Gauis* Book XXXVIII

Temple to the ground and in three days raise the Temple from the ground. Both there and here, **He** speaks in the madness of metaphors **His** own idled and raving mind comprehendeth?

He claims to speak of the temple of **His** body! Metaphors foretell madness and are the poetic preenings of the lunatick. The Temple is made from finished stone, so that neither hammer nor axe nor any tool of iron is heard in the Temple. And **He** will dwell among the children of Israel, and will not forsake **His** people Israel. So Solomon built the Temple, and finished it. The body is not the Temple! We are not the temple of **God**, and the **Spirit of God** dwelleth not in us. Doth **His** disciples believeth they are the temple of the living **God**? for they believeth **God** said, **"I will dwell in them, and walk in them; and I will be their God, and they shall be My people."**

Fie! Dwell in us? Walk in us! They are twisting and distorting! David **His** servant shall be king over us; and we all shall have one shepherd: we shall also walk in **His** judgments, and observe **His** statutes, and do them. And we shall dwell in the land that **He** have given unto Jacob **His** servant, wherein our fathers have dwelt; and we shall dwell therein, even we, and our children, and our children's children for ever: and **His** servant David shall be their prince for ever. Moreover **He** will make a covenant of peace with us; it shall be an everlasting covenant with us: and **He** will place us, and multiply us, and will set **His** Temple in the midst of us for evermore. **He** makes **His** dwelling place with us (not in us); yea, **He** will be our **God**, and we shall be **His** people. And the heathen shall know that **He,** the **Lord**, doth sanctify Israel, when **His** Temple shall be in the midst of us for evermore.

His disciples, under **His** tutelage shalt seek to rob **His**

unavoidable grave of **His** body upon the third day so that these words suggest **He** is risen! His **false Messiah** shalt force the hands of the chief priests and the Pharisees to come together in unity unto Pilate, following the day of the preparation, and say, "Sir, we remember that that deceiver said, while he was yet alive, **'After three days I will rise again.'** Command therefore that the sepulchre be made sure until the third day, lest his disciples come by night, and steal him away, and say unto the people, 'Be not affrighted: Ye seek **Jesus of Nazareth**, which was crucified: **He** is risen; **He** is not here': so the last error shall be worse than the first."

Wilt they say, "Blessed be the **God** and **Father** of our **Lord Jesus Christ**, which according to **His** abundant mercy hath begotten us again unto a lively hope by the resurrection of **Jesus Christ** from the dead, to an inheritance incorruptible, and undefiled, and that fadeth not away, reserved in heaven for you,who are kept by the power of **God** through faith unto salvation ready to be revealed in the last time."

Wilt they say, "Now if we be dead with **Christ**, we believe that we shall also live with **Him**: Knowing that **Christ** being raised from the dead dieth no more; death hath no more dominion over **Him**. For in that **He** died, **He** died unto sin once: but in that **He** liveth, **He** liveth unto God. Likewise reckon ye also yourselves to be dead indeed unto sin, but alive unto **God** through **Jesus Christ our Lord**."

And wilt they pray, "The **God** of our **Lord Jesus Christ**, the **Father of glory**, may give unto you the spirit of wisdom and revelation in the knowledge of **Him**: The eyes of your understanding being enlightened; that ye may know what is the hope of **His** calling, and what the riches of the glory of his inheritance in the saints, and what is the

His disciples steal into His tomb to steal His body under the cover of the darkness of night!

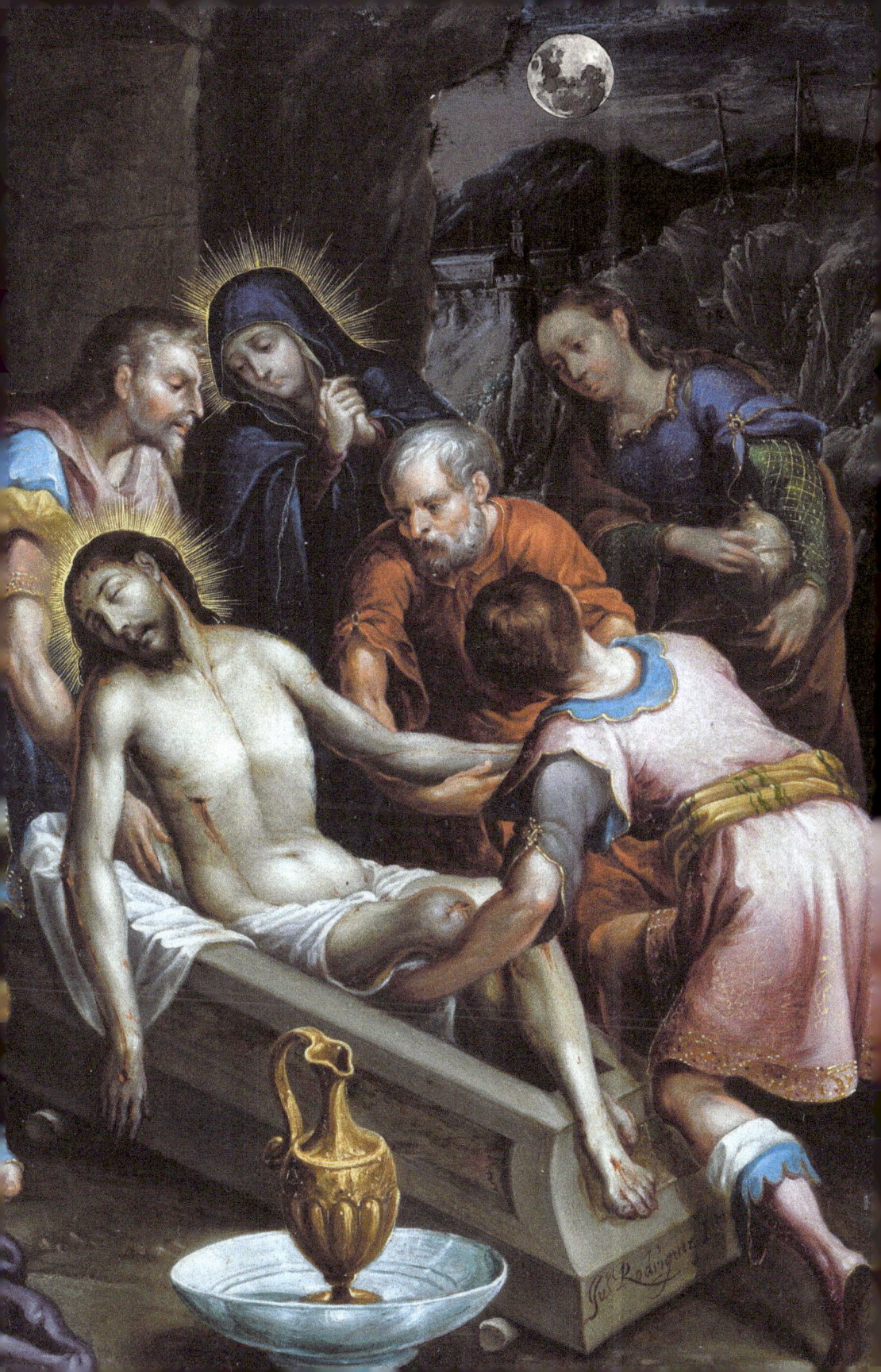

exceeding greatness of **His** power to us-ward who believe, according to the working of **His** mighty power, which **He** wrought in **Christ**, when **He** raised **Him** from the dead, and set **Him** at **His** own right hand in the heavenly places, far above all principality, and power, and might, and dominion, and every name that is named, not only in this world, but also in that which is to come: and hath put all things under **His** feet, and gave **Him** to be the head over all things to the church, which is **Him** body, the fulness of **Him** that filleth all in all."

And wilt they at the end of the world say, "And from **Jesus Christ**, who is the faithful witness, and the first begotten of the dead, and the prince of the kings of the earth. Unto **Him** that loved us, and washed us from our sins in **His** own blood, and hath made us kings and priests unto **God** and **His Father**; to **Him** be glory and dominion for ever and ever."

And Pontius Pilate shalt honor our request for a guard and saith unto us, "Ye have a watch: go your way, make it as sure as ye can." So shalt we go, and made the sepulchre sure, sealing the stone, and setting a watch.

—I record these words after this report to his honourable Caiaphas was fulfilled to increase the fulness of its reporting. And if when it came to pass that disciples of **His** circumvented our guard, and behold, some of the watch came into the city, and shewed unto the chief priests all the things that were done:

Now upon the first day of the week, very early in the morning, the women of **His** discipleship came unto the sepulchre, bringing the spices which they had prepared, and certain others with them. And they found the stone rolled away from the sepulchre. And they entered in, and found not the body of their **Lord** for it had been stolen in the night by the men of **His** discipleship. And it came to pass, as they were much perplexed thereabout, behold, two men stood by them in white garments (secret hidden disciples?): and as the women were afraid, and bowed down their faces to the earth, they said unto them, "Why seek ye the living among the dead? **He** is not here, but is risen: remember how **He** spake unto you when **He** was yet in Galilee, saying, '**The Son of man must be delivered into the hands of sinful men, and be crucified, and the third day rise again.**' " And they remembered **His** words, and returned from the sepulchre, and told all these things unto the eleven, and to all the rest. It was Mary Magdalene and Joanna, and Mary the mother of James, and other women that were with them, which told these things unto the apostles. And women believed their words fell onto the disciples them as the idle tales rash talking women tell, and **His** disciples believed the women not. They believed them not for they had stolen into the rich man's tomb shrouded in the darkness of the night to removeth the **His** body and give rise to the rumours of a risen **Christ**.

And when we assembled with the elders, and had to take counsel, we gave large money unto the soldiers for keeping their guard, saying, "Say ye, '**His** disciples came by night, and stole him away while we slept.' Which they surely did by some machination and deception unknown to us. "And when this come to the governor's ears, we persuaded him, and secure you." So they took the money, and did as they were taught: and this saying is commonly reported among the Jews until this day.—

We must scheme in our dreams to defeat and destroy this false-faced Messiah! Only a **false Messiah** premeditatedly fulfils the prophecies of the **LORD God of Israel** and purposefully pursues **His** own death by crucifixion at the hands of Pontius Pilate to self-fulfil **His** own fraudulent prophecies to that one may grow **His** own reignition and renown amongst **His** trifling band of disciples. Absurdities laid on the foundation of madness!

When they were come to Capernaum, they that received tribute money came to Peter, and said, "Doth not your **Master** pay tribute?" He saith, "Yes." And when he was come into the house, **He** prevented him, saying, **"What thinkest thou, Simon? of whom do the kings of the earth take custom or tribute? of their own children, or of strangers?"** Peter saith unto **Him**, "Of strangers." **He** saith unto him, **"Then are the children free. Notwithstanding, lest we should offend them, go thou to the sea, and cast an hook, and take up the fish that first cometh up; and when thou hast opened his mouth, thou shalt find a piece of money: that take, and give unto them for Me and thee."** And Peter did as he was bade and fished the coin out of the fish's mouth. What manner of conjury is this? Such delightful deceptions mayest entertain Herod Antipas, his wife Herodias, and his court, but the elders and the chief priests and the scribes knoweth the chicanery of the conjuring charlatan when we encounter **Him**.

And when **He** came to Capernaum: and being in the house **He** asked them, "What was it that ye disputed among yourselves by the way?" But they held their peace: for whilst on the journey to Capernaum, the disciples hath during the length of their travel squabbled amongst themselves far from **His** ear as to who should be the greatest. Andrew spake first inciting the quarrel, "Was not I a disciple of the Baptist? Hath I not yearned for the coming of **Christ**? Of ye disciples, I was but the first!" And Peter saith in response, "I am the rock on which is built **His** church! I walked on water. Trust is my reward." James the Greater saith inflaming the quarrel, "Ha! swifty fled thy faith and into the brisk sea thee drowned! Was not I there with thee and my brother when our **Lord** was trans-figured? I saw Moses Lawgiver and Elias and radiant light from the **Messiah**. Like thee, I beheld a bright cloud over-shadowed us: and behold a voice out of the cloud, which said, 'This is my beloved Son, in whom I am well pleased; hear ye Him.' " "Am not I, John, called by **Him** the Belov-ed, who can claim the sight of Jairus' daughter resurrected: traversing death's water." Then saith Bartholomew, "Am not I likewise called disciple of the Baptist?" James the Lesser ruked, "Didst ye not say no good comes from Nazareth?" And Thomas saith, "I spake, 'Let us go! we may die with **Him**!' " Then James the Lesser saith, "Ye question, argue, and doubt is thy sin!" And Judas, the one who will betray **Him**, saith, "I believeth the Messiah wields a sword! Shalt I force **His** hand to fulfill the **Word**!? To extirpate the weeds of Roman dogs from a militant Messiah!" And Matthew saith, "I shalt of the Good News be chronicler." And James the Lesser rebuked, "Fie! ye art the bane! a tax collector!"

Remembeth the **LORD** saith, "I lay in Zion for a foundation a stone, a tried stone, a precious corner stone, a sure foundation: he that believeth shall not make haste." **His** ministry is built upon the foundation of the apostles and prophets, with **Himself** being the chief corner stone; in whom all the building fitly framed together groweth unto an holy temple in the **Lord**: in whom also are builded together for an habitation of **God** through the **Spirit**. And yet I witnessed the very cracks formeth in the foundation stones that shalt topple the whole of **His** ministry into rubble upon the ground.

And **He** sat down, and called the twelve, and saith unto them, **"If any man desire to be first, the same shall be last of all, and servant of all."** And **He** called a little child unto **Him**, and set **Him** in the midst of them, and said, **"Verily I say unto you, except ye be converted, and become as little children, ye shall not enter into the kingdom of heaven. Whosoever therefore shall humble himself as this little child, the same is greatest in the kingdom of heaven. Whosoever shall receive one of such children in My name, receiveth Me: and whosoever shall receive Me, receiveth not Me, but Him that sent Me."**

Now the Jews' feast of tabernacles was at hand. **His** brethren therefore said unto **Him**, "Depart hence, and go into Judaea, that **Thy** disciples also may see the works that **Thou** doest. For there is no man that doeth any thing in secret, and he himself seeketh to be known openly. If **Thou** do these things, shew **Thyself** to the world." For neither did **His** brethren believe in **Him**. **His** brethren or kinsmen of were disgusted, when they found there was no prospect of worldly advantages from him. Ungodly men sometimes undertake to counsel those employed in the work of God; but they only advise what appears likely to promote present advantages. The people differed about **His** doctrine and miracles, while those who favoured **Him**, dared not openly to avow their sentiments.[2]

Then **He** said unto them, **"My time is not yet come:**

2   Henry, Matthew, *Commentary on the Whole Bible*, abridged

but your time is alway ready. The world cannot hate you; but Me it hateth, because I testify of it, that the works thereof are evil. Go ye up unto this feast: I go not up yet unto this feast: for My time is not yet full come." When He had said these words unto them, He abode still in Galilee. ✝

Chapter 9
"Bless the Adulteress"

O THE TEMPLE HE CAME AGAIN in the early morning, and all the people came unto **Him**; and **He** sat down, and taught them. And the scribes and Pharisees brought unto **Him** a woman taken in adultery. Let her exposure as an wanton adulteress be a warning to all as the LORD saith, "For the lips of a strange woman drop as an honeycomb, and her mouth is smoother than oil: But her end is bitter as wormwood, sharp as a two-edged sword. Her feet go down to death; her steps take hold on hell. Lest thou shouldest ponder the path of life, her ways are moveable, that thou canst not know them. Hear me now therefore, O! ye children, and depart not from the words of my mouth. Remove thy way far from her, and come not nigh the door of her house: lest thou give thine honour unto others, and thy years unto the cruel: lest strangers be filled

with thy wealth; and thy labours be in the house of a stranger; and thou mourn at the last, when thy flesh and thy body are consumed, And say, how have I hated instruction, and my heart despised reproof; and have not obeyed the voice of my teachers, nor inclined mine ear to them that instructed me! I was almost in all evil in the midst of the congregation and assembly. Drink waters out of thine own cistern, and running waters out of thine own well. Let thy fountains be dispersed abroad, and rivers of waters in the streets. Let them be only thine own, and not strangers' with thee. Let thy fountain be blessed: and rejoice with the wife of thy youth. Let her be as the loving hind and pleasant roe; let her breasts satisfy thee at all times; and be thou ravished always with her love. And why wilt thou, my son, be ravished with a strange woman, and embrace the bosom of a stranger?"

And when my brethren had set the beguiling strange woman in **His** midst, we said unto **Him**, "**Master**, this woman was taken in adultery, in the very obscene act, laying back her with her neighbour betwixt her thighs, defiling her husband's marriage bed; her exuberant moaning and groaning sounded an alarm that altered her neighbours, whom informed the elders and the chief priests and the scribes to her sinful crime. Now! Moses Lawgiver in the Law commanded us, the man that committeth adultery with another man's wife, even he that committeth adultery with his neighbour's wife, the adulterer and the adulteress shall surely be put to death: but what sayest **Thou**?"

This we said, tempting **Him**, that we might have to accuse **Him**. Time and time again doth **He** rewrite, reinterpret, and revolt against the Laws bequeathed unto us by Moses Lawgiver. Now, in the Temple, with the audience of

His faithful multitude, we seeketh to expose this **false Messiah** whom often and awfully blasphemes against Laws of the **LORD God of Israel**. But **He** stooped down, and with his finger wrote on the ground, as though **He** heard us not.

So when my brethren continued asking **Him**, "It is heard amongst those from the Galilee and the town of Nazareth that **Thy** own mother, espoused to Joseph, wast accused of adultery being found with child, but Joseph her husband, **Thy** father, being a just man, and not willing to make her a publick example, was minded to put her away privily. But gossiping hens within Nazareth saith, 'An angel of the **LORD** appeared unto him in a dream, saying, "Joseph, thou son of David, fear not to take unto thee Mary thy wife: for that which is conceived in her is of the **Holy Ghost**. And she shall bring forth a **Son**, and thou shalt call his name **Jesus**: for **He** shall save **His** people from their sins." ' "

He lifted up himself, and said unto them, **"He that is without sin among you, let him first cast a stone at her."** And again **He** stooped down, and wrote on the ground. And we which heard it, being convicted by our own conscience, went out one by one, beginning at the eldest, even unto the last: and **He** was left alone (with a few of **His** disciples), and the woman standing in the midst. When **He** had lifted up **Himself**, and saw none but the woman, **He** said unto her, **"Woman, where are those thine accusers? hath no man condemned thee?"** She said, "No man, **Lord**." And **He** said unto her, **"Neither do I condemn thee: go, and sin no more."**

In His blasphemy, He blesses the adulteress rather than obey the Law of the LORD!

Then spake **He** again unto them, saying, **"I am the light of the world: he that followeth Me shall not walk in darkness, but shall have the light of life."** Is this false **Christ** the Light of the world? **God** is light, and **He** claimeth to be the image of the invisible **God**. One sun enlightens the whole world; so does this one **Christ**? There needs no more than one! What a dark dungeon would the world be without the sun! For the **LORD God** is a sun and shield: the **LORD** will give grace and glory: no good thing will **He** withhold from them that walk uprightly. Those who follow **Christ** shall walk in darkness. They shall be left without the truths which are necessary to keep them from destroying error, and the directions in the way of duty, necessary to keep them from condemning sin.[1]

The Pharisees therefore said unto **Him**, "**Thou** bearest record of **Thyself**; **Thy** record is not true." For we are learned in the Law: one witness shall not rise up against a man for any iniquity, or for any sin, in any sin that he sinneth: at the mouth of two witnesses, or at the mouth of three witnesses, shall the matter be established. **He** answered and said unto them, **"Though I bear record of Myself, yet My record is true: for I know whence I came, and whither I go; but ye cannot tell whence I come, and whither I go."** And again and again **He** spake and more and more false doctrines fell from **His** lips. **"Ye judge after the flesh; I judge no man. And yet if I judge, My judgment is true: for I am not alone, but I and the Father that sent Me. It is also written in your law, that the testimony of two men is true. I**

---

1   Henry, Matthew, *Commentary on the Whole Bible*, abridged, paraphrased

am one that bear witness of Myself, and the Father that sent Me beareth witness of Me." Should we knew **Christ** better? we knoweth the **Father** better. Those become vain in their imaginations concerning **God**, who will learn of **Christ** instead. Those who know not **His** glory and grace, know the **Father** sent **Him** not.
2

  Then said my brethren unto **Him**, "Where is **Thy Father**?" **He** answered, **"Ye neither know Me, nor My Father: if ye had known Me, ye should have known My Father also."** These words spake **He** in the treasury, as **He** taught in the temple: and no man laid hands on **Him**; for we possessed not the evidence yet and the time had not yet come to proceed. Howbeit when this record is complete, shall we render unto Caesar a seditionist and Messianic threat against Rome, and then and only then mayest **He** be crucified under the yoke of the prefect of Judaea, Pontius Pilate.

  Then said **He** again unto my brethren, **"I go My way, and ye shall seek Me, and shall die in your sins: whither I go, ye cannot come."** Then said the Jews, "Will **He** kill **Himself**? because **He** saith, '**Whither I go, ye cannot come.'** " And **He** said unto them, **"Ye are from beneath; I am from above: ye are of this world; I am not of this world. I said therefore unto you, that ye shall die in your sins: for if ye believe not that I am he, ye shall die in your sins."** Then said they unto **Him**, "Who art **Thou**?"

  And **He** saith unto them, **"Even the same that I said unto you from the beginning. I have many things to say and to judge of you: but He that sent Me is true; and I speak to the world those things which I have heard of Him. When ye have lifted up the Son of man, then shall**

2 Henry, Matthew, *Commentary on the Whole Bible*, abridged, paraphrased

ye know that I am He, and that I do nothing of myself; but as My Father hath taught Me, I speak these things. And He that sent Me is with Me: the Father hath not left Me alone; for I do always those things that please Him."

Those that live in unbelief, are for ever undone, if they die in unbelief. The Jews belonged to this present world, but **He** believeth **He** is of a heavenly and Divine nature, so that **His** doctrine, kingdom, and blessings, would not suit our taste. But **He** believeth our Law is a curse done away to all that submit to the grace of **His** gospel. **He** believeth nothing but the doctrine of **Christ's** grace will be an argument powerful enough, and none but the **Spirit** of **Christ's** grace will be an agent powerful enough, to turn us from sin to **God**; and that **Spirit** is given, and that doctrine is given, to work upon those only who believe in **Christ**. But who is this **Jesus**? **His** disciples allow **Him** to deceive them into believing **He** to have been a Prophet, an excellent Teacher, and even more than a creature! But we cannot and must acknowledge **Him** as over all, **God** blessed for evermore. This shall not suffice for **Him**! Is this to honour **Him** as the **Father**? Does this admit **His** being the **Light of the world**, and the **Life of men**, one with the **Father**? All shall know by their deception into conversion, or in their condemnation for not converting, that **He** always spake and did what **He** saith pleased the **Father**, even when **He** claimed the highest honours for **Himself**![3]

As **He** spake these words, many incompetent men believed on **Him**. Then said **He** to those Jews which foolishly believed on him, **"If ye continue in My word, then are ye My disciples indeed; And ye shall know the truth, and the truth shall make you free."** They answered **Him**, **"We**

---

3 Henry, Matthew, *Commentary on the Whole Bible*, abridged, paraphrased

be Abraham's seed, and were never in bondage to any man: how sayest thou, Ye shall be made free?"

He answered them, "**Verily, verily, I say unto you, whosoever committeth sin is the servant of sin. And the servant abideth not in the house for ever: but the Son abideth ever. If the Son therefore shall make you free, ye shall be free indeed. I know that ye are Abraham's seed; but ye seek to kill Me, because My word hath no place in you. I speak that which I have seen with My Father: and ye do that which ye have seen with your father.**"

They answered and said unto Him, "Abraham is our father." He saith unto them, "**If ye were Abraham's children, ye would do the works of Abraham. But now ye seek to kill Me, a Man that hath told you the truth, which I have heard of God: this did not Abraham. Ye do the deeds of your father.**" Then said they to Him, "We be not born of fornication; we have one Father, even God."

This false **Christ** opposed the proud confidence of my brethren, showing that our descent from Abraham could not profit those of a contrary spirit to **Him**. Where the Law of Moses has no place, no good is to be expected; room is left there for all wickedness. A sick person who turns from his physician, and will take neither remedies nor food, is past hope of recovery. The truth both heals and nourishes the hearts of those who receive it. The truth taught by philosophers has not this power and effect, but only the truth of **God**. We who claim the privileges of Abraham, must do Abraham's works; must be strangers and sojourners in this world; keep up the worship of **God** in our families, and always walk before **God**.[4]

He said unto them, "**If God were your Father, ye**

---

4   Henry, Matthew, *Commentary on the Whole Bible*, abridged, paraphrased

would love Me: for I proceeded forth and came from God; neither came I of Myself, but He sent Me. Why do ye not understand My speech? even because ye cannot hear My word. Ye are of your father the devil, and the lusts of your father ye will do. He was a murderer from the beginning, and abode not in the truth, because there is no truth in him. When he speaketh a lie, he speaketh of his own: for he is a liar, and the father of it. And because I tell you the truth, ye believe Me not. Which of you convinceth Me of sin? And if I say the truth, why do ye not believe Me? He that is of God heareth God's words: ye therefore hear them not, because ye are not of God."

Then answered the Jews, and said unto **Him**, "Say we not well that **Thou** art a Samaritan, and hast a devil?" Satan prompts men to excesses by which they murder themselves and others, while what he puts into the mind tends to ruin men's souls. He is the great promoter of falsehood of every kind. He is a liar, all his temptations are carried on by his calling evil good, and good evil, and promising freedom in sin. He is the author of all lies; whom liars resemble and obey, with whom all liars shall have their portion for ever. The special lusts of the devil are spiritual wickedness, the lusts of the mind, and corrupt reasonings, pride and envy, wrath and malice, enmity to good, and enticing others to evil. By the truth, here understand the revealed will of God as by the Torah, the Nev'im, and the Ketuvim and not to the salvation of men by Jesus Christ, the lies Christ was now preaching, and which the Jews opposed.[5]

He smiled and answered, "**I have not a devil; but I honour My Father, and ye do dishonour Me. And I seek not Mine own glory: there is one that seeketh and**

---

5 Henry, Matthew, *Commentary on the Whole Bible*, abridged, paraphrased

judgeth. Verily, verily, I say unto you, if a man keep My saying, he shall never see death.”

Then said the Jews unto **Him**, “Now we know that **Thou** hast a devil. Abraham is dead, and the prophets; and **Thou** sayest, ‘If a man keep My saying, he shall never taste of death.’ Art thou greater than our father Abraham, which is dead? and the prophets are dead: whom makest thou thyself?” He answered smiling, **“If I honour Myself, My honour is nothing: it is My Father that honoureth Me; of whom ye say, that He is your God: Yet ye have not known Him; but I know Him: and if I should say, I know Him not, I shall be a liar like unto you: but I know Him, and keep his saying. Your father Abraham rejoiced to see My day: and he saw it, and was glad.”**

Then said the Jews unto **Him**, “Thou art not yet fifty years old, and hast thou seen Abraham?” **He** said unto them, **“Verily, verily, I say unto you, before Abraham was, I AM.”** Then took they up stones to cast at him because they knoweth the knowledge that Moses asketh of **God**, “Behold, when I come unto the children of Israel, and shall say unto them, the **God** of your fathers hath sent me unto you; and they shall say to me, ‘What is his name?’ what shall I say unto them?” and! **God** said unto Moses, **‘I AM THAT I AM’** and **He** said, **‘Thus shalt thou say unto the children of Israel, I AM hath sent me unto you.’** ” Howbeit **He** hid **Himself**, and went out of the temple, going through the midst of them with the magicks of Beelezebub, and so passed by unmolested.

Chapter 10
"Belittle the Spittle"

S HE PASSED BY, HE SAW A MAN which was blind from his birth. And **His** disciples asked **Him**, saying, "Master, who did sin, this man, or his parents, that he was born blind?" For **His** disciples knoweth the Law that the **LORD** saith, "For I the LORD thy God am a jealous God, visiting the iniquity of the fathers upon the children unto the third and fourth generation of them that hate Me; and shewing mercy unto thousands of them that love Me, and keep My commandments."

He answered, "Neither hath this man sinned, nor his parents: but that the works of God should be made manifest in him. I must work the works of him that sent Me, while it is day: the night cometh, when no man can work. As long as I am in the world, I am the light of the world."

118

When **He** had thus spoken, **He** spat on the ground, and made clay of the spittle, and **He** anointed the eyes of the blind man with the clay, so that it may be fulfilled that the eyes of the blind shall be opened, and the ears of the deaf shall be unstopped. And **He** said unto him, **"Go, wash in the pool of Siloam,"** (which is by interpretation, 'Sent'.) Just as when Naaman came with his horses and with his chariot, and stood at the door of the house of Elisha. And Elisha sent a messenger unto him, saying, "Go and wash in Jordan seven times, and thy flesh shall come again to thee, and thou shalt be clean." But Naaman was wroth, and went away, and said," Behold, I thought, he will surely come out to me, and stand, and call on the name of the **LORD** his **God**, and strike his hand over the place, and recover the leper. Are not Abana and Pharpar, rivers of Damascus, better than all the waters of Israel? may I not wash in them, and be clean? So he turned and went away in a rage. And his servants came near, and spake unto him, and said, "My father, if the prophet had bid thee do some great thing, wouldest thou not have done it? how much rather then, when he saith to thee, 'Wash', and be clean?" Then went he down, and dipped himself seven times in Jordan, according to the saying of the man of **God**: and his flesh came again like unto the flesh of a little child, and he was clean.

The blind man then went his way therefore, and washed, and came seeing. The neighbours therefore, and they which before had seen him that he was blind, said, "Is not this he that sat and begged? Some said, "This is he": others said, "He is like him": but he said, "I am he."

Therefore said they unto him, "How were thine eyes opened?" He answered and said, "A man that is called **Jesus of Nazareth of the Galilee** made clay, and anointed mine

eyes, and said unto me, 'Go to the pool of Siloam, and wash': and I went and washed, and I received sight. Then said they unto him, "Where is He?" He said, "I know not."

They brought to the Pharisees him that aforetime was blind. And it was the sabbath day when He made the clay, and opened his eyes. Then again the Pharisees also asked him how he had received his sight. He said unto them, "He put clay upon mine eyes, and I washed, and do see." Therefore said some of the Pharisees, "This man is not of God, because he keepeth not the sabbath day." Others said, "How can a man that is a sinner do such miracles?" And there was a division among my breathren.

They say unto the blind man again, "What sayest thou of Him, that He hath opened thine eyes? He said, "He is a prophet." And the blind man believeth that the LORD his God raised up unto him a Prophet from his very mist, of his brethren. But my brethren did not believe concerning him, that he had been blind, and received his sight, until they called the parents of him that had received his sight.

And the Pharisees asked them, saying, "Is this your son, who ye say was born blind? how then doth he now see?" His parents answered them and said, "We know that this is our son, and that he was born blind: But by what means he now seeth, we know not; or who hath opened his eyes, we know not: he is of age; ask him: he shall speak for himself." These words spake his parents, because they rightfully feared brethren: for the decree had been sent far and wide, that if any man did confess that He was Christ, he should be put out of the synagogue. Therefore said his parents, "He is of age; ask him." Then again called they the man that was blind, and said unto him, "Give God the praise": we know

He time and time against violated the sabbath and Law of the LORD!

that this **Man** is a sinner! For thus saith the **LORD of hosts,** **"Hearken not unto the words of the prophets that prophesy unto you: they make you vain: they speak a vision of their own heart, and not out of the mouth of the LORD."**

And the blind man answered and said, "Whether he be a sinner or no, I know not: one thing I know, that, whereas I was blind, now I see." Then said they to him again, "What did **He** to thee? how opened **He** thine eyes?" And the blind man answered them," I have told you already, and ye did not hear: wherefore would ye hear it again? will ye also be his disciples?"

Then my brethren rightfully reviled him, and said, "Thou art **His** disciple; but we are Moses' disciples. We know that God spake unto Moses: as for this fellow, we know not from whence **He** is." The man answered and said unto them, "Why herein is a marvellous thing, that ye know not from whence he is, and yet he hath opened mine eyes. Now we know that **God** heareth not sinners, for **He** saith, **'When you spread out your hands in prayer, I will hide My eyes from you; even though you multiply your prayers, I will not listen. Your hands are covered with blood.'** But if any man be a worshipper of God, and doeth his will, him he heareth. Since the world began was it not heard that any man opened the eyes of one that was born blind. If this man were not of **God**, he could do nothing."

They answered and said unto him, "Thou wast altogether born in sins, and dost thou teach us?" And they cast him out. And the blind man rebuked the Pharisees, "Now, hear the word of the **LORD**, ye that tremble at his word, **'Your brethren that hated You, that cast You out for My name's sake, said, "Let the LORD be glorified: but He shall appear to Your joy", and they shall be ashamed.'"**

He heard that they had cast the now sighted man out; and when **He** had found him, **He** said unto him, "**Dost thou believe on the Son of God?**" The sighted man answered and said, "Who is **He**, **Lord**, that I might believe on **Him**?

And **He** said unto him, "**Thou hast both seen Him, and it is He that talketh with thee.**" And he said, "**Lord**, I believe." And he worshipped **Him**. And then **He** said, "**For judgment I am come into this world, the elders and the chief priests and the scribes that accusest thee dwellest in the midst of a rebellious house, which have eyes to see, and see not; they have ears to hear, and hear not: for they are a rebellious house. Thou which do not see will see, that they which see might be made blind.**"

And some of my breathren which were with **Him** heard these words, and said unto **Him**, "Are we blind also?" **He** said unto them, "**If ye were blind, ye should have no sin: but now ye say, 'We see'; therefore your sin remaineth. Behold, thou art called a Jew, and restest in the law, and makest thy boast of God, and knowest His will, and approvest the things that are more excellent, being instructed out of the Law; and art confident that thou thyself art a guide of the blind, a light of them which are in darkness, an instructor of the foolish, a teacher of babes, which hast the form of knowledge and of the truth in the Law. Thou therefore which teachest another, teachest thou not thyself? thou that preachest a man should not steal, dost thou steal? Thou that sayest a man should not commit adultery, dost thou commit adultery? thou that abhorrest idols, dost thou commit sacrilege? Thou that makest thy boast of the law, through breaking the law dishonourest thou God? For the name of God is blasphemed among the Gentiles through you, as it is written.**"

"Verily, verily, I say unto you, he that entereth not by the door into the sheepfold, but climbeth up some other way, the same is a thief and a robber. But he that entereth in by the door is the shepherd of the sheep. To him the porter openeth; and the sheep hear his voice: and he calleth his own sheep by name, and leadeth them out. And when he putteth forth his own sheep, he goeth before them, and the sheep follow him: for they know his voice. And a stranger will they not follow, but will flee from him: for they know not the voice of strangers."

This parable spake **He** unto my brethren: but they understood not what things they were which **He** spake unto them. Then said **He** unto them again, "Verily, verily, I say unto you, I am the door of the sheep. All that ever came before Me are thieves and robbers: but the sheep did not hear them. I am the door: by Me if any man enter in, he shall be saved, and shall go in and out, and find pasture. The thief cometh not, but for to steal, and to kill, and to destroy: I am come that they might have life, and that they might have it more abundantly.

"I am the good shepherd: the good shepherd giveth His life for the sheep. But he that is an hireling, and not the shepherd, whose own the sheep are not, seeth the wolf coming, and leaveth the sheep, and fleeth: and the wolf catcheth them, and scattereth the sheep. The hireling fleeth, because he is an hireling, and careth not for the sheep. I am the good shepherd, and know My sheep, and am known of Mine. As the Father knoweth Me, even so know I the Father: and I lay down My life for the sheep. And other sheep I have, which are not of this fold: them also I must bring, and they shall hear My voice; and there shall be one fold, and one shepherd.

"Therefore doth My Father love Me, because I lay down My life, that I might take it again. No man taketh it from Me, but I lay it down of Myself. I have power to lay it down, and I have power to take it again. This commandment have I received of My Father." There was a division therefore again among the Jews for these sayings. And many of them said, "He hath a devil, and is mad; why hear ye Him?" Others said, "These are not the words of Him that hath a devil. Can a devil open the eyes of the blind?"

And it was at Jerusalem the feast of the dedication, and it was winter. And He walked in the temple in Solomon's porch. Then came the Jews round about Him, and said unto Him, "How long dost Thou make us to doubt? If thou be the Christ, tell us plainly." He answered them, "I told you, and ye believed not: the works that I do in My Father's name, they bear witness of Me. But ye believe not, because ye are not of My sheep, as I said unto you. My sheep hear My voice, and I know them, and they follow Me: and I give unto them eternal life; and they shall never perish, neither shall any man pluck them out of My hand. My Father, which gave them Me, is greater than all; and no man is able to pluck them out of My Father's hand. I and My Father are One."

Fie! Thus saith the LORD! "I AM the Lord, and there is none else, there is no God beside me: I girded thee, though thou hast not known Me: that they may know from the rising of the sun, and from the west, that there is none beside me. I AM the Lord, and there is none else. I form the light, and create darkness: I make peace, and create evil: I the Lord do all these things." and! "I AM the first, and I AM the last; and beside Me there is no God." and! "Remember the former things of old: for I AM God, and there is none else; I AM God, and there is none like Me."

So then my brethren took up stones again to stone **Him**. He answered them, **"Many good works have I shewed you from My Father; for which of those works do ye stone Me?"** My brethren answered **Him**, saying, "For a good work we stone **Thee** not; but for blasphemy; and because that **Thou**, being a man, makest **Thyself** God".

He answered them, **"Is it not written in your Law, I said 'Ye are gods'? If he called them gods, unto whom the word of God came, and the scripture cannot be broken; Say ye of Him, whom the Father hath sanctified, and sent into the world, 'Thou blasphemest'; because I said, 'I AM the Son of God?' If I do not the works of My Father, believe Me not. But if I do, though ye believe not Me, believe the works: that ye may know, and believe, that the Father is in Me, and I in Him."**

Is it not written? Is it not written! Fie Is it not written in our Law concerning the redeemer: "Ye are my witnesses and My servant whom I have chosen: that ye may know and believe Me, and understand that I am He: before Me there was no God formed, neither shall there be after Me. I, even I, am the LORD; and beside Me there is no saviour."

Therefore they sought again to take him: but **He** escaped out of their hand, and went away again beyond Jordan into the place where John at first baptized; and there **He** abode. And many resorted unto **Him**, and said, "John did no miracle: but all things that John spake of this **Man** were true." And many believed on **Him** there. ✝

Chapter 11
"The Seditionary Seventy"

FTER THESE THINGS HE AP-
pointed other seventy also, and sent them
two and two before **His** face into every city
and place, whither **He Himself** would come.
And these are the seventy **He** named (that ye, O! honourable
Caiaphas, mayest set our network of spies upon them all):

James the Lord's brother; Cleopas; Simeon, son of
Cleopas, second bishop of Jerusalem; Matthias; Thadde-
us of Edessa; Stephen, one of the Seven Deacons, the first
martyr; Philip, who baptized the eunuch, one of the Seven
Deacons, bishop of Tralles in Asia Minor; Prochorus, one of
the Seven Deacons, bishop of Nicomedia in Bithynia; Nica-
nor the Deacon, one of the Seven Deacons; Timon, one of
the Seven Deacons; Parmenas the Deacon, one of the Seven
Deacons; Barnabas, companion of Paul; Mark the Evangelist, and bishop of Alexandria; Luke the Evangelist;

Agabus the Prophet; Amplias Justus, bishop of Eleutheropolis; Ananias, bishop of Damascus; Timothy, bishop of Ephesus; Titus, bishop of Crete; Philemon, bishop of Gaza; Onesimus; Epaphras, bishop of Andriaca; Archippus; Silas, bishop of Corinth; Silvanus; Crescens; Crispus, bishop of Chalcedon in Galilee; Epenetus, bishop of Carthage; Andronicus, bishop of Pannonia; Stachys, bishop of Byzantium; Amplias, bishop of Odissa; Urban, bishop of Macedonia; Narcissus, bishop of Athens; Apelles, bishop of Heraklion; Aristobulus, bishop of Britain; Herodion, bishop of Patras; Rufus, bishop of Thebes; Asyncritus, bishop of Hyrcania; Phlegon, bishop of Marathon; Hermes, bishop of Philippopolis; Parrobus, bishop of Pottole; Hermas, bishop of Dalmatia; Pope Linus, bishop of Rome; Gaius, bishop of Ephesus; Philologus, bishop of Sinope; Lucius of Cyrene, bishop of Laodicea in Syria; Jason, bishop of Tarsus; Sosipater, bishop of Iconium; Olympas; Tertius, bishop of Iconium; Erastus, bishop of Paneas; Quartus, bishop of Berytus; Euodias, bishop of Antioch; Onesiphorus, bishop of Cyrene; Clement, bishop of Sardis; Sosthenes, bishop of Colophon; Apollos, bishop of Caesarea; Tychicus, bishop of Colophon; Epaphroditus; Carpus, bishop of Beroea in Thrace; Quadratus; Zenas the Lawyer, bishop of Diospolis; Aristarchus, bishop of Apamea in Syria; Pudens; Trophimus; Mark, bishop of Apollonia; Artemas, bishop of Lystra; Aquila; Fortunatus; Achaicus; Tabitha, a woman disciple, whom Peter raised from the dead; and Caleb, circumcised the eighth day, of the stock of Israel, of the tribe of Levi, an Hebrew of the Hebrews; as touching the law, a Pharisee of Pharisees whom honours Moses Lawgiver and a spy within the ministry of **Jesus of Nazareth of the Galilee**.

Therefore said **He** unto all of the seventy, **"The har-**

vest truly is great, but the labourers are few: pray ye therefore the Lord of the harvest, that He would send forth labourers into His harvest. Go your ways: behold, I send you forth as lambs among wolves. Carry neither purse, nor scrip, nor shoes: and salute no man by the way. And into whatsoever house ye enter, first say, 'Peace be to this house.' And if the Son of peace be there, your peace shall rest upon it: if not, it shall turn to you again. And in the same house remain, eating and drinking such things as they give: for the labourer is worthy of his hire. Go not from house to house. And into whatsoever city ye enter, and they receive you, eat such things as are set before you: and heal the sick that are therein, and say unto them, 'The kingdom of God is come nigh unto you.'

"But into whatsoever city ye enter, and they receive you not, go your ways out into the streets of the same, and say, 'Even the very dust of your city, which cleaveth on us, we do wipe off against you: notwithstanding be ye sure of this, that the kingdom of God is come nigh unto you.' But I say unto you, that it shall be more tolerable in that day for Sodom, than for that city. Woe unto thee, Chorazin! woe unto thee, Bethsaida! for if the mighty works had been done in Tyre and Sidon, which have been done in you, they had a great while ago repented, sitting in sackcloth and ashes. But it shall be more tolerable for Tyre and Sidon at the judgment, than for you. And thou, Capernaum, which art exalted to heaven, shalt be thrust down to hell. He that heareth you heareth Me; and he that despiseth you despiseth Me; and he that despiseth Me despiseth him that sent Me."

And the seventy returned again with joy, saying, "Lord, even the devils are subject unto us through Thy name." And

He said unto them, "Lo! I beheld him as lightning fall from heaven and the great dragon was cast out, that old serpent, called the Devil, and Satan, which deceiveth the whole world: he was cast out into the earth, and his angels were cast out with him. O! How art thou fallen from heaven, Lucifer, son of the morning! how art thou cut down to the ground, which didst weaken the nations! For thou hast said in thine heart, 'I will ascend into heaven, I will exalt My throne above the stars of God: I will sit also upon the mount of the congregation, in the sides of the north.'

"Behold! thou shalt tread upon the lion and adder: the young lion and the dragon shalt thou trample under feet, and over all the power of the enemy: and nothing shall by any means hurt you. Notwithstanding in this rejoice not, that the spirits are subject unto you; but rather rejoice, because your names are written in heaven. And thy enemies let them be blotted out of the book of the living, and not be written with the righteous.

"But! not every one that saith unto Me, 'Lord, Lord,' shall enter into the kingdom of heaven; but he that doeth the will of My Father which is in heaven. Many will say to Me in that day, 'Lord, Lord, have we not prophesied in Thy name? and in Thy name have cast out devils? and in thy name done many wonderful works?' And then will I profess unto them, I never knew you: depart from Me, ye that work iniquity."

In that hour He rejoiced in spirit, and said, "I thank Thee, O! Father, Lord of heaven and earth, that Thou hast hid these things from the wise and prudent, and hast revealed them unto babes: even so, Father; for so it seemed good in Thy sight. All things are delivered to Me of My Father: and no man knoweth who the Son is, but the Father; and who the Father is, but the Son, and he to whom the Son will reveal Him."

And He turned Him unto He disciples, and said privately, "Blessed are the eyes which see the things that ye see: for I tell you, that many prophets and kings have desired to see those things which ye see, and have not seen them; and to hear those things which ye hear, and have not heard them.

"Assured am I that the prophets have inquired and searched diligently, who prophesied of the grace that should come unto you: searching what, or what manner of time the Spirit of Christ which was in them did signify, when it testified beforehand My sufferings of, and the glory that should follow. Unto whom it was revealed, that not unto themselves, but unto them shalt ye minister the things, which are now reported unto them by you that have preached the gospel unto them with the Holy Ghost sent down from heaven; which things the angels desire to look into. Wherefore gird up the loins of your mind, be sober, and hope to the end for the grace that is to be brought unto you at My revelation."

And, behold, a certain lawyer stood up, and tempted him, saying, "Master, what shall I do to inherit eternal life?" He said unto him, "What is written in the law? how readest thou?" And he answering said, "Thou shalt love the LORD thy God with all thine heart, and with all thy soul, and with all thy might; but if from thence thou shalt seek the LORD thy God, thou shalt find Him, if thou seek Him with all thy heart and with all thy soul; if thou doth hearken diligently unto **His** commandments which **He** command thee this day, to love the **LORD** thy **God**, and to serve **Him** with all thy heart and with all thy soul then **He** will send grass in thy fields for thy cattle, that thou mayest eat and be full; if thou hearken diligently unto the voice of the **LORD** your **God**, to observe and to do all **His** commandments which **He** commands thee this day, that the **LORD** your **God** will set thee on high above all nations of the earth; and thou shalt not avenge, nor bear any grudge against the children of thy people, but thou shalt love thy neighbour as thyself."

And **He** said unto him, **"Thou hast answered right: My Father commanded us to do all these statutes, to fear the My Father, for our good always, that He might preserve us alive, as it is at this day. He that keepeth the commandment keepeth his own soul; but he that despiseth His ways shall die."** But he, willing to justify himself, said unto **Him**, "And who is my neighbour?" And **He** answering said:

"A certain man went down from Jerusalem to Jericho, and fell among thieves, which stripped him of his raiment, and wounded him, and departed, leaving him half dead. And by chance there came down a certain priest that way: and when he saw him, he passed by on the other side. *Is it not to deal thy bread to the hungry, and that thou bring the poor that are cast out to thy house? when thou seest the naked, that thou cover him; and that thou hide not thyself from thine own flesh?* **And likewise a Levite, when he was at the place, came and looked on him, and passed by on the other side.** *Is it not to deal thy bread to the hungry, and that thou bring the poor that are cast out to thy house? when thou seest the naked,*

A reviled and vile Samaritan dishonours his nation by assisting the wounded man!

that thou cover him; and that thou hide not thyself from thine own flesh? But a certain Samaritan, as he journeyed, came where he was: and when he saw him, he had compassion on him, And went to him, and bound up his wounds, pouring in oil and wine, and set him on his own beast, and brought him to an inn, and took care of him. And on the morrow when he departed, he took out two pence, and gave them to the host, and said unto him, Take care of him; and whatsoever thou spendest more, when I come again, I will repay thee. Which now of these three, thinkest thou, was neighbour unto him that fell among the thieves?"

And the lawyer said, "He that shewed mercy on him." Then said He unto him, "Go, and do thou likewise."

Now it came to pass, as they went, that He entered into a certain village: and a certain woman named Martha received Him into her house. And she had a sister called Mary, which also sat at His feet, (Yea! He loved the people; all His saints are in His hand: and they sat down at His feet; every one shall receive of His words) and heard His word:

"And Elisha came again to Gilgal: and there was a dearth in the land; and the sons of the prophets were sitting before him: and he said unto his servant, 'Set on the great pot, and seethe pottage for the sons of the prophets.' And one went out into the field to gather herbs, and found a wild vine, and gathered thereof wild gourds his lap full, and came and shred them into the pot of pottage: for they knew them not. So they poured out for the men to eat. And it came to pass, as they were eating of the pottage, that they cried out, and said, "O! thou man of God, there is death in the pot.' And they could not eat thereof. But he said, 'Then bring meal.' And he

---

He visits two of His most devoted and deceived sycophants, the sisters Mary and Mary!

cast it into the pot; and he said, 'Pour out for the people', that they may eat. And there was no harm in the pot."

But Martha was cumbered about much serving, and came to **Him**, and said, "**Lord**, dost **Thou** not care that my sister hath left me to serve alone? bid her therefore that she help me." And **He** answered and said unto her, **"Martha, Martha, thou art careful and troubled about many things: But one thing is needful: and Mary hath chosen that good part, which shall not be taken away from her."**

Chapter 12
"The Blackest Sabbaths"

E CAST OUT A DEVIL, AND IT was dumb, so that it might be fulfilled what Isaiah spake, "The lame man leap as an hart, and the tongue of the dumb sing: for in the wilderness shall waters break out, and streams in the desert."

When the devil was gone out, the dumb spake: "He that dwelleth in the secret place of the **Most High** shall abide under the shadow of the **Almighty**. I will say of the **LORD**, '**He** is my refuge and my fortress: **My God**; in **Him** will I trust.' Surely **He** shall deliver thee from the snare of the fowler, and from the noisome pestilence. **He** shall cover thee with **His** feathers, and under **His** wings shalt thou trust: **His** truth shall be thy shield and buckler. Thou shalt not be afraid for the terror by night; nor for the arrow that flieth by day; nor for the pestilence that walketh in darkness; nor for the destruction that wasteth at noonday. A thousand shall fall at thy side, and ten thousand at thy right hand; but it shall not come nigh thee. Only with thine eyes shalt thou behold and see the reward of the wicked. Because thou hast made the LORD, which is my refuge, even the Most High, thy habitation; There shall no evil befall thee, neither shall any plague come nigh thy dwelling. For He shall give His angels charge over thee, to keep thee in all thy ways. They shall bear thee up in their hands, lest thou dash thy foot against a stone. Thou shalt tread upon the lion and adder: the young lion and the dragon shalt thou trample under feet. 'Because he hath set his love upon Me, therefore will I deliver him: I will set him on high, because he hath known My name. He shall call upon Me, and I will answer him: I will be with him in trouble; I will deliver him, and honour him. With long life will I satisfy him, and shew him My salvation.' "

And the people wondered. But some of them said, "He casteth out devils through Beelzebub the chief of the devils."

And others, tempting Him, saying, "When Thy fame went throughout all Syria: and the people brought unto Thee all sick people that were taken with divers diseases and torments, and those which were possessed with devils, and those which were lunatick, and those that had the palsy; and Thou healed them." They sought of Him a sign from heaven. But He, knowing their thoughts, said unto them:

"Every kingdom divided against itself is brought to desolation; and a house divided against a house falleth. If Satan also be divided against himself, how shall his kingdom stand? because ye say that I cast out devils through Beelzebub. And if I by Beelzebub cast out devils, by whom do your sons cast them out? therefore shall they be your judges. But if I with the finger of God cast out devils, no doubt the kingdom of God is come upon you. When a strong man armed keepeth his palace, his goods are in peace: But when a stronger than he shall come upon him, and overcome him, he taketh from him all his armour wherein he trusted, and divideth his spoils. He that is not with Me is against Me: and he that gathereth not with Me scattereth.

"When the unclean spirit is gone out of a man, he walketh through dry places, seeking rest; and finding none, he saith, 'I will return unto my house whence I came out.' And when he cometh, he findeth it swept and garnished. Then goeth he, and taketh to him seven other spirits more wicked than himself; and they enter in, and dwell there: and the last state of that man is worse than the first."

And when the people were gathered thick together, He began to say, "This is an evil generation: they seek a sign; and there shall no sign be given it, but the sign of Jonas the prophet. For as Jonas was a sign unto the Ninevites, when he began to enter into the city a day's journey, and he cried, and said, 'Yet forty days, and Nineveh shall be overthrown,' so shall also the Son of man be to this generation. when the queen of Sheba heard of the fame of Solomon, she came to prove Solomon with hard questions at Jerusalem, with a very great company, and camels that bare spices, and gold in abundance, and precious stones: and when she was come to Solomon, she communed with him of all that was in her heart and she shall rise up in the judgment with the men of this generation, and condemn them: for she came from the utmost parts of the earth to hear the wisdom of Solomon; and, behold, a greater than Solomon is here. The men of Nineve, who believed God, and proclaimed a fast, and put on sackcloth, from the greatest of them even to the least of them, shall rise up in the judgment with this generation, and shall condemn it: for they repented at the preaching of Jonas; and, behold, a greater than Jonas is here."

And as **He** spake, a certain Pharisee besought **Him** to dine with him: and **He** went in, and sat down to meat. And when the Pharisee saw it, **He** marvelled that **He** had not first washed before dinner. The Pharisee knoweth the Law that the **LORD** spake unto Moses Lawgiver, saying, "Thou shalt also make a laver of brass, and his foot also of brass, to wash withal: and thou shalt put it between the tabernacle of the congregation and the altar, and thou shalt put water therein. For Aaron and his sons shall wash their hands and their feet thereat: when they go into the tabernacle of the congregation, they shall wash with water, that they die not; or when they come near to the altar to minister, to burn offering made by fire unto the Lord: So they shall wash their hands and their feet, that they die not: and it shall be a statute for ever to them, even to him and to his seed throughout their generations."

The Pharisee rebuked **Him** by praying thus, "Blessed are **Thou**, O! **Lord**, our **God**, **King of the Universe**, **Who** has sanctified us through **Thy** commandments and has commanded us concerning the washing of hands."

And the **He** said unto him, "The scribes and the Pharisees sit in Moses' seat: All therefore whatsoever they bid

The Pharisees suffer the abuse of an obtuse sermon!)

you observe, that observe and do; but do not ye after their works: for they say, and do not. For they bind heavy burdens and grievous to be borne, and lay them on men's shoulders; but they themselves will not move them with one of their fingers. But all their works they do for to be seen of men: they make broad their phylacteries, and enlarge the borders of their garments, And love the uppermost rooms at feasts, and the chief seats in the synagogues, And greetings in the markets, and to be called of men, 'Rabbi, Rabbi.' But be not ye called Rabbi: for one is your Master, even Christ; and all ye are brethren. And call no man your father upon the earth: for one is your Father, which is in heaven. Neither be ye called masters: for one is your Master, even Christ. But he that is greatest among you shall be your servant. And whosoever shall exalt himself shall be abased; and he that shall humble himself shall be exalted. But–

"Woe! unto you, scribes and Pharisees, hypocrites! for ye shut up the kingdom of heaven against men: for ye neither go in yourselves, neither suffer ye them that are entering to go in. Woe! unto you, scribes and Pharisees, hypocrites! for ye devour widows' houses, and for a pretence make long prayer: therefore ye shall receive the greater damnation.

"Woe! unto you, scribes and Pharisees, hypocrites! for ye compass sea and land to make one proselyte, and when he is made, ye make him twofold more the child of hell than yourselves.

"Woe! unto you, ye blind guides, which say, 'Whosoever shall swear by the temple, it is nothing; but whosoever shall swear by the gold of the temple, he is a debtor!' Ye fools and blind: for whether is greater, the gold, or the temple that sanctifieth the gold? And, 'Whosoever shall swear by the altar, it is nothing; but whosoever sweareth by the gift that is upon it, he is guilty.' Ye fools and blind: for whether is greater, the gift, or the altar that sanctifieth the gift? Whoso therefore shall swear by the altar, sweareth by it, and by all things thereon. And whoso shall swear by the temple, sweareth by it, and by him that dwelleth therein. And he that shall swear by heaven, sweareth by the throne of God, and by him that sitteth thereon.

"Woe! unto you, scribes and Pharisees, hypocrites! for ye pay tithe of mint and anise and cummin, and have omitted the weightier matters of the law, judgment, mercy, and faith: these ought ye to have done, and not to leave the other undone. Ye blind guides, which strain at a gnat, and swallow a camel.

"Woe! unto you, scribes and Pharisees, hypocrites! for ye make clean the outside of the cup and of the platter, but within they are full of extortion and excess. Thou blind Pharisee, cleanse first that which is within the cup and platter, that the outside of them may be clean also.

"Woe! unto you, scribes and Pharisees, hypocrites! for ye are like unto whited sepulchres, which indeed appear beautiful outward, but are within full of dead men's bones, and of all uncleanness. Even so ye also outwardly appear righteous unto men, but within ye are full of hypocrisy and iniquity.

"Woe! unto you, scribes and Pharisees, hypocrites! because ye build the tombs of the prophets, and garnish the sepulchres of the righteous, And say, 'If we had been in the days of our fathers, we would not have been partakers with them in the blood of the prophets.'

"Wherefore ye be witnesses unto yourselves, that ye are the children of them which killed the prophets. Fill ye up then the measure of your fathers. Ye serpents, ye generation of vipers, how can ye escape the damnation of hell? Wherefore, behold, I send unto you prophets, and wise men, and scribes: and some of them ye shall kill and crucify; and some of them shall ye scourge in your synagogues, and persecute them from city to city: That upon you may come all the righteous blood shed upon the earth, from the blood of righteous Abel unto the blood of Zacharias son of Barachias, whom ye slew between the temple and the altar. Verily I say unto you, All these things shall come upon this generation.

"O! Jerusalem, Jerusalem, thou that killest the prophets, and stonest them which are sent unto thee, how often would I have gathered thy children together, even as a hen gathereth her chickens under her wings, and ye would not! Behold, your house is left unto you desolate. For I say unto you, Ye shall not see Me henceforth, till ye shall say, 'Blessed is he that cometh in the name of the Lord.' "

And as He said these things unto them, the scribes and the Pharisees began to urge Him vehemently, and to provoke Him to speak of many things: laying wait for Him, and seeking to catch something out of His mouth, that they might accuse Him.

And He was teaching in one of the synagogues on the sabbath. And, behold, there was a woman which had a spirit of infirmity eighteen years, and was bowed together, and could in no wise lift up herself. And when He saw her,

He called her to **Him**, and said unto her, "Woman, thou art loosed from thine infirmity." And **He** laid **His** hands on her: and immediately she was made straight, and glorified **God**.

And the ruler of the synagogue answered with indignation, because that **He** had healed on the sabbath day, and said unto the people, as the elders and the chief priests and scribes spake unto the children of Israel, saying, "Verily my sabbaths ye shall keep: for it is a sign between me and you throughout your generations; that ye may know that I am the Lord that doth sanctify you. Ye shall keep the sabbath therefore; for it is holy unto you: every one that defileth it shall surely be put to death: for whosoever doeth any work therein, that soul shall be cut off from among his people. Six days may work be done; but in the seventh is the sabbath of rest, holy to the Lord: whosoever doeth any work in the sabbath day, he shall surely be put to death. Wherefore the children of Israel shall keep the sabbath, to observe the sabbath throughout their generations, for a perpetual covenant. It is a sign between me and the children of Israel for ever: for in six days the Lord made heaven and earth, and on the seventh day he rested, and was refreshed."

He then answered him, and said, "Thou hypocrite, doth not each one of you on the sabbath loose his ox or his ass from the stall, and lead him away to watering? And ought not this woman, being a daughter of Abraham, whom Satan hath bound, lo, these eighteen years, be loosed from this bond on the sabbath day?" And when **He** had said these things, all **His** adversaries were ashamed: and all the people rejoiced for all the glorious things that were done by **Him**.

Then said **He**, "Unto what is the kingdom of God

like? and whereunto shall I resemble it? It is like a grain of mustard seed, which a man took, and cast into his garden; and it grew, and waxed a great tree; and the fowls of the air lodged in the branches of it." And again He said, "Whereunto shall I liken the kingdom of God? It is like leaven, which a woman took and hid in three measures of meal, till the whole was leavened."

And it was at Jerusalem the feast of the dedication, and it was winter. And He walked in the temple in Solomon's porch. Then came the Jews round about Him, and said unto Him, "How long dost Thou make us to doubt? If thou be the Christ, tell us plainly." Yay! Finally...

He answered them, "I told you, and ye believed not: the works that I do in My Father's name, they bear witness of Me. But ye believe not, because ye are not of My sheep, as I said unto you. My sheep hear My voice, and I know them, and they follow Me: And I give unto them eternal life; and they shall never perish, neither shall any man pluck them out of My hand. My Father, which gave them Me, is greater than all; and no man is able to pluck them out of My Father's hand. I and My Father are one."

Then the Jews took up stones again to stone Him. He answered them, "Many good works have I shewed you from My Father; for which of those works do ye stone Me?" The Jews answered Him, saying, "For a good work we stone Thee not; but for blasphemy; and because that Thou, being a man, makest Thyself God."

He answered them, "Is it not written in your law, 'I said, "Ye are gods?"' If He called them gods, unto whom the word of God came, and the Scripture cannot be broken; say ye of Him, whom the Father hath sanctified, and sent into the world, 'Thou blasphemes't; because I said, 'I AM the Son of God'? If I do not the works of My Father, believe Me not. But if I do, though ye believe not Me, believe the works: that ye may know, and believe, that the Father is in Me, and I in Him." Therefore they sought again to take him: but he escaped out of their hand.

And went away again beyond Jordan into the place where John at first baptized; and there **He** abode. And many resorted unto **Him**, and said, "John did no miracle: but all things that John spake of this **Man** were true." And many believed on **Him** there.

Chapter 13
"The Righteous Plot to Kill Jesus"

S HE WENT INTO THE HOUSE of one of the chief Pharisees to eat bread on the sabbath day, that my brethren watched **Him**. And, behold, there was a certain man brought before **Him** which had the dropsy. And **He** answering spake unto the lawyers and Pharisees, saying, **"Is it lawful to heal on the sabbath day?"** Howbeit they held their peace.

Then **He** took him which had the dropsy, and healed him, and let him go; and answered the lawyers, saying, **"Is it lawful to removeth debris to save a life on the sabbath, and the more eager one is, the more praiseworthy art thou; doth thou obtain permission of the Sanhedrin? How so? If thou saw a child falling into the sea, thou spread a net and bring it up— the faster the better, doth thee need obtain permission of the Sanhedrin though he**

thereby catches fish in his net? If thee saw a child fall into a pit, thou breaketh loose one segment of the entrenchment and pulls it up– the faster the better; doth thou need obtain permission of the Sanhedrin, even though he is thereby making stairs. If thou saw a door closing upon an infant, thou mayest break it, so as to get the child out– the faster the better; and he need not obtain permission from the Sanhedrin, though thou thereby consciously makes chips of wood? Mayest thou extinguish and isolate the fire in the case of a conflagration– the sooner the better, and thou need not obtain permission from the Sanhedrin, even though thou subdues the flames?"[1]

Now the elders and the chief priests and the scribes knoweth in all these cases must be mentioned separately. For if only the case of the infant falling into the sea had been mentioned thou would have said, it is permitted there because meantime the child might be swept away by the water, but that doth not apply in the case of its falling into the pit, because since the child remains stays therein, thou might have thought, thou may not save it before obtaining permission, therefore it is necessary to refer to that. And if the teaching had confined itself to the case of the pit, thou would have thought, there no permission is required because the child is terrified but in the case of a door closing upon it, thou might sit outside and amuse the child by making a noise with nuts, therefore it was necessary to include that too.[1] We knoweth these things yet my brethren did not entertain to answer **Him** again to these things.

And there went great multitudes with **Him**: and **He** turned, and said unto them, **"If any man come to Me, and hate not his father, and mother, and wife, and children,**

---

1   The Babylonian Talmud - Mas. Yoma 84b

and brethren, and sisters, yea, and his own life also, he cannot be My disciple. And whosoever doth not bear his cross, and come after Me, cannot be My disciple. For which of you, intending to build a tower, sitteth not down first, and counteth the cost, whether he have sufficient to finish it? Lest haply, after he hath laid the foundation, and is not able to finish it, all that behold it begin to mock him, saying, 'This man began to build, and was not able to finish.' Or what king, going to make war against another king, sitteth not down first, and consulteth whether he be able with ten thousand to meet him that cometh against him with twenty thousand? Or else, while the other is yet a great way off, he sendeth an ambassage, and desireth conditions of peace. So likewise, whosoever he be of you that forsaketh not all that he hath, he cannot be My disciple.

"Salt is good: but if the salt have lost his savour, wherewith shall it be seasoned? It is neither fit for the land, nor yet for the dunghill; but men cast it out. He that hath ears to hear, let him hear."

Then drew near unto Him all the publicans and sinners for to hear Him. And the Pharisees and scribes murmured, saying, 'This Man receiveth sinners, and eateth with them'. Who art the men which thanketh Him their Lord, who hath enabled them, for that He counted them faithful, putting them into His ministry; who was before a blasphemer, and a persecutor, and injurious: but they obtained mercy, because they did it ignorantly in unbelief? And who was the grace of their Lord exceeding abundant with faith and love which is in Him? This is a condemnable saying, and worthy of all rejection, that He came into the world to save sinners; of whom many art chief. Howbeit for this cause they obtained mercy, that in they first He might shew forth all longsuffering, for a pattern to them which should hereafter believe on **Him** to life everlasting; now unto the **King** eternal, immortal, invisible, the only wise **God**, be honour and glory for ever and ever? Fie!

And **He** spake this parable unto them, saying: "**What man of you, having an hundred sheep, if he lose one of them, doth not leave the ninety and nine in the wilderness, and go after that which is lost, until he find it? And when he hath found it, he layeth it on his shoulders, rejoicing. And when he cometh home, he calleth together his friends and neighbours, saying unto them, 'Rejoice with me; for I have found My sheep which was lost!' I say unto you, that likewise joy shall be in heaven over one sinner that repenteth, more than over ninety and nine just persons, which need no repentance.**

"**Either what woman having ten pieces of silver, if she lose one piece, doth not light a candle, and sweep the house, and seek diligently till she find it? And when she hath found it, she calleth her friends and her neighbours together, saying, 'Rejoice with me; for I have found the piece which I had lost.' Likewise, I say unto you, there is joy in the presence of the angels of God over one sinner that repenteth.**"

And! He said, "**A certain man had two sons: And the younger of them said to his father, 'Father, give me the portion of goods that falleth to me.' And he divided unto them his living. And not many days after the younger son gathered all together, and took his journey into a far country, and there wasted his substance with riotous living. And when he had spent all, there arose a mighty famine in that land; and he began to be in want. And he went and joined himself to a citizen of that country; and** he sent him into his fields to feed swine. And he would fain have filled his belly with the husks that the swine did eat: and no man gave unto him.

"And when he came to himself, he said, 'How many hired servants of my father's have bread enough and to spare, and I perish with hunger! I will arise and go to my father, and will say unto him, "Father, I have sinned against heaven, and before thee, And am no more worthy to be called thy son: make me as one of thy hired servants." '

"And he arose, and came to his father. But when he was yet a great way off, his father saw him, and had compassion, and ran, and fell on his neck, and kissed him. And the son said unto him, 'Father, I have sinned against heaven, and in thy sight, and am no more worthy to be called thy son.'

"But the father said to his servants, 'Bring forth the best robe, and put it on him; and put a ring on his hand, and shoes on his feet: And bring hither the fatted calf, and kill it; and let us eat, and be merry: For this my son was dead, and is alive again; he was lost, and is found.' And they began to be merry.

"Now his elder son was in the field: and as he came and drew nigh to the house, he heard musick and dancing. And he called one of the servants, and asked what these things meant. And he said unto him, 'Thy brother is come; and thy father hath killed the fatted calf, because he hath received him safe and sound.'

And he was angry, and would not go in: therefore came his father out, and intreated him. And he answering said to his father, 'Lo, these many years do I serve thee, neither transgressed I at any time thy commandment: and yet thou never gavest me a kid, that I might make merry with my friends: but as soon as this thy son was come, which hath devoured thy living with harlots, thou hast killed for him the fatted calf.'

"And he said unto him, 'Son, thou art ever with me, and all that I have is thine. It was meet that we should make merry, and be glad: for this thy brother was dead, and is alive again; and was lost, and is found.' "

Now a certain man was sick, named Lazarus, of Bethany, the town of Mary and her sister Martha. (It was that Mary which anointed the Lord with ointment, and wiped his feet with her hair, whose brother Lazarus was sick.) Therefore his sisters sent unto **Him**, saying, "**Lord**, behold, he whom **Thou** lovest is sick." When He heard that, He said, "**This sickness is not unto death, but for the glory of God, that the Son of God might be glorified thereby.**" Now **He** loved Martha, and her sister, and Lazarus. When **He** had heard therefore that **He** was sick, **He** abode two days still in the same place where **He** was. Then after that saith he to his disciples, "**Let us go into Judaea again.**"

His disciples say unto **Him**, "**Master**, the Jews of late sought to stone Thee; and goest **Thou** thither again?" **He** answered, "**Are there not twelve hours in the day? If any man walk in the day, he stumbleth not, because he seeth the light of this world. But if a man walk in the night, he stumbleth, because there is no light in him.**" These things said **He**: and after that **He** saith unto them, "**Our friend Lazarus sleepeth; but I go, that I may awake him out of sleep.**"

Then said **His** disciples, "**Lord**, if he sleep, he shall do well." Howbeit **He** spake of his death: but they thought that **He** had spoken of taking of rest in sleep. Then said **He** unto them plainly, "**Lazarus is dead. And I am glad for your sakes that I was not there, to the intent ye may believe; nevertheless let us go unto him.**"

Then said Thomas, which is called Didymus, unto **His** fellow disciples, "Let us also go, that we may die with **Him**."

Then when **He** came, **He** found that he had lain in the grave four days already. Now Bethany was nigh unto Jerusalem, about fifteen furlongs off: and many of the Jews came to Martha and Mary, to comfort them concerning their brother. Then Martha, as soon as she heard that **He** was coming, went and met **Him**: but Mary sat still in the house. Then said Martha unto **Him**, "**Lord**, if **Thou** hadst been here, my brother had not died." She clapped **Him** again and again upon **His** cheeks and buffeted **Him** upon **His** chest with her fists. "But I know," she continueth that even now, whatsoever **Thou** wilt ask of **God**, **God** will give it **Thee**." **He** saith unto her, "**Thy brother shall rise again.**" Martha saith unto **Him**, "I know that he shall rise again in the resurrection at the last day." **He** said unto her, "**I am the resurrection, and the life: he that believeth in Me, though he were dead, yet shall he live: And whosoever liveth and believeth in Me shall never die. Believest thou in Me?**"

She saith unto **Him**, "Yea, **Lord**: I believe that **Thou** art the **Christ**, the **Son of God**, which should come into the world." And when she had so said, she went her way, and called Mary her sister secretly, saying, "The **Master** is come, and calleth for thee." As soon as she heard that, she arose quickly, and came unto **Him**. Now **He** was not yet come into the town, but was in that place where Martha met **Him**. The Jews then which were with her in the house, and comforted her, when they saw Mary, that she rose up hastily and went out, followed her, saying, 'She goeth unto the grave to weep there.'

Then when Mary was come where **He** was, and saw **Him**, she fell down at his feet, saying unto **Him**, "**Lord**, if **Thou** hadst been here, my brother had not died." When **He** therefore saw her weeping, and the Jews also weeping which came with her, **He** groaned in the spirit, and was troubled. And said, **"Where have ye laid him?"**

They said unto **Him**, "**Lord**, come and see." **He** wept. Then said the Jews, "Behold how **He** loved him!" And some of them said, "Could not this **Man**, which opened the eyes of the blind, have caused that even this man should not have died?"

He therefore again groaning in **Himself** cometh to the grave. It was a cave, and a stone lay upon it. **He** said, **"Take ye away the stone."** Martha, the sister of him that was dead, saith unto him, "**Lord**, by this time he stinketh: for he hath been dead four days." **He** saith unto her, **"Said I not unto thee, that, if thou wouldest believe, thou shouldest see the glory of God?"**

Then they took away the stone from the place where the dead was laid. And **He** lifted up his eyes, and said, **"Father, I thank Thee that Thou hast heard Me. And I knew that Thou hearest Me always: but because of the people which stand by I said it, that they may believe that Thou hast sent Me."** And when he thus had spoken, **He** cried with a loud voice, **"Lazarus, come forth."** And he that was dead came forth, bound hand and foot with graveclothes: and his face was bound about with a napkin. **He** saith unto them, **"Loose him, and let him go."**

Then many of the Jews which came to Mary, and had

seen the things which **He** did, believed on **Him**. But some of them went their ways to the Pharisees, and told them what things **He** had done. Then gathered the chief priests and the Pharisees a council, and said, "What do we? for this **Man** doeth many miracles. If we let **Him** thus alone, all men will believe on **Him**: and the Romans shall come and take away both our place and nation."

And thee O! honourable Caiaphas, being the high priest that same year, said unto them, "Ye know nothing at all, Nor consider that it is expedient for us, that one **Man** should die for the people, and that the whole nation perish not." And this spake he not of himself: but being high priest that year, he prophesied that Jesus should die for that nation; And not for that nation only, but that also he should gather together in one the children of God that were scattered abroad.

Then from that day forth we took counsel together for to put **Him** to death. **He** therefore walked no more openly among the Jews; but went thence unto a country where we lost Him into the wilderness. But there continued with **His** disciples.

And the Jews' passover was nigh at hand: and many went out of the country up to Jerusalem before the passover, to purify themselves. Then sought we for **Him**, and spake among ourselves, as we stood in the temple, "What think ye, that **He** will not come to the feast?" Now both the chief priests and the Pharisees had given a commandment, that, if any man knew where **He** were, he should shew it, that they might take **Him**.

And! I sewed dissension and betrayal in the very tapestry of **His** ministry turning one called Judas Iscariot, whom said, "What will ye give me, Pharisee, and I will deliver **Him** unto you?" And I covenanted with him for thirty pieces of

silver; so that **His** disciples couldst add one last fulfilment of prophecy to **His** list: for Zechariah saith, "If
ye think good, give me my price; and if not, forbear.
So they weighed for my price thirty pieces of silver. And
the **LORD** said unto me, **'Cast it unto the potter: a
goodly price that I was prised at of them.'** And I took
the thirty pieces of silver, and cast them to the potter in
the house of the **LORD**." And from that time he sought
opportunity to betray **Him**.

Howbeit, forasmuch as many have taken in hand to
watch the purported Messiah, **Jesus, the son of Joseph of
Nazareth of the Galilee**, the Sanhedrin from the very beginning sent forth spies, that I have feigned myself **His** disciple, that I took hold of **His** words and **His** deeds, which
from the very beginning of **His** ministry reeked of blasphemy, witnessed by and influencing many into rebuking our
authority, and sowing dissension amongst the multitudes
against us and thereby I delivereth this report **His** words and
His deeds to you, most exalted Caiaphas, that you might
deliver **Him** unto the power and authority of the governor,
Pontius Pilate. Amen.

The Gospels of Biblical Horror
Trinity

Book 3

The Machination of Vipers
978-1-931608-71-8
$15.00

Book 2

Book 1

The First Exorcist / The Harrowing of the Inferno
Special FLIPable Printing
ISBN: 978-1-931608-60-2
$17.00

The Harrowed Heart
978-1-931608-48-0
$15.00

Artwork Bibliography

Bassano, Jacopo, *The Good Samaritan*, c. 1562-63, National Gallery, London

Bloch, Carl, *The Sermon on the Mount*, 1877, The Museum of National History, Hillerød, Denmark

Bridges, John *Healing Peter's mother-in-law*, 1839, Birmingham Museum of Art, Birmingham, Alabama

Cranach, Lucas The Younger, *Christ and the Adulteress,* after 1532, Hermitage Museum, St. Petersburg, Russia

Ciseri, Antonio, *Ecce Homo (Behold the Man!)*, 1871

da Lodi, Callisto Piazza, *Beheading of St. John the Baptist*, Galleria dell Accademia, Venice

de Klerk, Hendrik, *The Feeding of the Five Thousand*

Jodaens, Jacob, *Christ Driving the Money Changers from the Temple,* c. 1650, Louvre Museu m, Paris, France

Juárez, Juan Rodríguez, *The Entombment of Christ*, c. 1702, The Metropolitan Museum of Art, New York City, New York

Munkácsy, Mihály, *Christ in front of Pilate,* 1881, Déri Museum, Debrecen, Hungary

Rembrandt, *Judas returning the thirty silver pieces,* 1629, Mulgrave Castle, Lythe, North Yorkshire

Rubens, Peter Paul, *The Elevation of the Cross*, 1610-11

Stettner, Georg Friedrich, *Christ in the House of Martha*, c. 17th century

Theotokopoulos, Domenikos (El Greco), *Christ Cleansing the Temple*, c 16th Century, National Gallery of ARt, Washington D.C., United States

Theotokopoulos, Domenikos "El Greco", *Christ Healing the Blind*, c. 1570, The Metropolitan Museum, New York City

Tissot, James, *The Calling of Peter and Andrew*, c. 1886-94, Brooklyn Museum, New York

Tissot, James, *The Flight of the Prisoners* c. 1896-1902.

Tissot, James, *Jesus Unrolls the Book in the Synagogue*, c. 1886-94, Brooklyn Museum, New York

van Scorel, Jan, *Mary Magdalene*, c. 1530, Rijksmuseum, Amsterdam, Netheralnds

Veronese, Paolo, *Jesus among the doctors*, c. 1560, Mesueo del Prado, Madrid, Spain

Veronese, Paolo, *Jesus and the Centurion*, c. 1571, Mesueo del Prado, Madrid, Spain

Veronese, Paolo, *The Baptism of Christ*, c 1580-88, Getty Center, Los Angeles, California

www.ingramcontent.com/pod-product-compliance
Lightning Source LLC
Chambersburg PA
CBHW071218260626
47162CB00004B/1342

* 9 7 8 1 9 3 1 6 0 8 7 1 8 *